THE HUNTSMAN

Superintendent Budd is faced with one of his toughest assignments in separating the strands of mystery that grip the village of Chalebury: a series of robberies perpetrated by the burglar known as Stocking-foot; sightings of the ghostly Huntsman; and the murders of a villager and a local police inspector. Interweaving with these is the suspicious behaviour of a frightened young woman who lives in a large dilapidated house with one elderly servant. Is there a connection between all these crimes and other oddities happening in the tiny village?

GERALD VERNER

THE HUNTSMAN

Complete and Unabridged

LINFORD
Leicester

First published in Great Britain

First Linford Edition
published 2017

A catalogue record for this book is available
from the British Library.

ISBN 978–1–4448–3529–8

1

The Legend

The new landlord of the Fox and Hounds, that rambling thirteenth-century inn which stands back from the Old Post Road on the outskirts of Chalebury, held the glass he had been polishing and examined it critically.

'I don't say there ain't such things as ghosts,' he remarked, 'but I do say it 'ud take more'n George Hickling's word to make me believe he saw one!'

''E swears 'e saw it plain, Mr. Ketler,' said a red-faced man, lifting a tankard of beer to his lips. 'Clear in the moonlight, on the crest of the 'ill by Newnham's Spinney.'

'I know what he says,' replied the sceptical Mr. Ketler, 'but it don't convince me, Mr. Bragg.'

'What time was it when 'e saw it?' asked a stocky man, a twinkle in his blue eyes.

Mr. Bragg swallowed a mouthful of his beer before replying, 'Jest arter eleven. 'E was on 'is way 'ome when he seen it.'

'Don't think George Hicklin' could see anythin' plain at that time o' night,' said the stocky man, and there was a general laugh.

'Imagination, that's what it were!' declared a voice from the other side of the low-ceilinged bar. 'The 'Untsman ain't been seen for fifty year or more.'

'You tell George that, Perkins!' retorted Mr. Bragg, pushing his tankard across the counter to be refilled. He looked across at the big-faced clock. ''E ought to be 'ere by now. Late ternight, ain't 'e?'

'Maybe it was one of the gentry out for a moonlight gallop,' suggested a mild little man in glasses.

'What, in 'untin' togs at that hour?' said the stocky man scornfully. 'Don't be goofy, Taplin! I'll bet George didn't see nothin'. It was the beer 'e'd 'ad playin' tricks on 'im.'

'I wouldn't like to say that, Scowby,' said Mr. Bragg, who had evidently constituted himself George Hickling's champion.

'As one of them writer fellers says, 'There's more things on the earth than what a man can dream about.' We didn't ought to disbelieve wot George Hicklin' says 'e saw, 'cause it ain't got a natural explanation.'

'I thought I'd given you one,' said Scowby with a grin.

'What I says,' continued Mr. Bragg, 'is that because the 'Untsman ain't been seen for over half a century, ain't no reason for, bein' sure 'e ain't turned up agin now.'

'You've quite gorn over to the spooks, 'aven't you, Bragg?' sneered Scowby, and a titter ran round the occupants of the bar.

'If you mean by that, do I believe in the 'Untsman, yes!' declared Mr. Bragg defiantly. 'And there's more in Chalebury what does, too, Tom Scowby!'

'Excuse me, gentlemen!' A man who had been sitting quietly at a table in the corner, drinking a whisky-and-soda and listening with interest to the conversation, broke in before the stickily built Scowby could reply. 'Who, or what, is the Huntsman?'

3

All eyes turned to the speaker. His face was big and square, his lips thin and uncompromising, the eyes penetrating beneath shaggy brows, the crisp hair splashed with grey. He wore a fleecy overcoat, which enhanced his breadth of shoulder and suggested opulence, for the cloth was of an expensive quality.

'A stranger in these parts, ain't you, sir?' Mr. Bragg asked, and when the other nodded: 'Thought so, otherwise you wouldn't 'ave to ask who the 'Untsman was.'

'Is he, or it, then, of local fame?' inquired the stranger.

'Well, yes,' said Mr. Bragg, 'though I should've thought most people would've 'eard of the 'Untsman of Chalebury.'

Mr. Ketler leaned forward, resting his shirt-sleeved arms on his bar. 'You tell us the story, Mr. Bragg,' he suggested. 'I've never 'eard the rights of it meself, although of course I've 'eard tell of the Huntsman.'

'It goes back a good few years,' said Mr. Bragg, gazing thoughtfully at the beer in his tankard. '1820, accordin' to all accounts. This was always a great place for fox 'unting — just as it is now — and a Chalebury 'as always been the M.F.H., like the present Sir Eustace is. At that time it was old Sir Thomas Chalebury who was the master, and a fair old devil 'e was, too, from the stories what 'ave been 'anded down about 'im. It's said 'e only 'ad two interests in life, 'unting and drinkin', and 'e could beat anybody else at either. There wasn't an 'orse nor a jump what could unseat 'im, and 'e could drink all 'is pals under the table.'

'In fact, a real old English gentleman,' murmured the stranger as Mr. Bragg paused to lubricate himself with another draught of beer.

'Yes, sir; I suppose that's what 'e'd 'ave been called in them days,' agreed Mr. Bragg, lowering his empty tankard. 'Well, arter a day's 'untin', this feller, Sir Thomas, and 'is friends used to go back to Chalebury Court and make a night of it, drinkin' and singin' till daybreak. It was during one of these horgies, so the story goes, that a servant, thinkin' they was all too drunk to spot 'im, made up 'is mind to clear off with what money and valuables 'e could lay 'is hands on.

'E got away, but 'e 'adn't been gorn more'n an hour before old Sir Thomas, who weren't so far gorn as 'is friends, discovered the robbery and swore 'e'd find the man and flay 'im alive. In a towerin' rage 'e called to 'is groom to saddle 'is 'orse and loose the 'ounds. 'E was still in 'is 'untin' clothes when 'e set off in the moonlight across country, with the 'ounds in full cry, singing 'John Peel' at the top of 'is voice, and cursin' the man who'd robbed 'im. 'E was never seen alive again. The 'ounds came back just as dawn was breakin' with their tails down and whimperin', and a search party set off to see what 'ad 'appened to their master. They found 'im near a place called Rackman's Wood, lyin' with a broken neck, beside the dead body of 'is 'orse. A few yards away was the servant 'e'd gorn arter, with 'is throat torn out.' Mr. Bragg paused impressively and eyed his attentive audience.

'There's been all sorts of people since who're s'posed to 'ave seen the ghost of old Sir Thomas gallopin' across country singin' 'John Peel',' he added. 'The legend goes that 'is appearance is a warnin' of death to the Chalebury family, or anyone what sees 'im.'

'Pretty bad look-out for George Hickling, then, ain't it?' Scowby remarked.

'It seems queer that George ain't been in yet,' said the little man with glasses.

'Oh, 'e'll come, sure as Christmas!' declared Perkins. 'There ain't nothing 'ud keep George away from 'is beer!'

The man in the fleecy coat rose to his feet, and his height was in keeping with the broadness of his chest.

'Thank you, Mr., er, Bragg,' he said, 'for a very interesting story. Perhaps in return you'll allow me to buy you a drink?'

'That's very kind of you, sir,' said the gratified Mr. Bragg. 'I'll have a pint of mild and bitter!'

'And you, gentlemen?' The stranger turned towards the other occupants of the bar. 'Will you join me?'

There was a chorus of thanks, and for the next few minutes Mr. Ketler was kept busy attending to his customers' demands.

'Well, 'ere's to your very good 'ealth, sir!' said Mr. Bragg. 'Are you stayin' in the neighbourhood?'

'I've bought White Cottage,' the stranger answered.

Mr. Ketler, in the act of shelving a bottle, looked round quickly, comprehension on his round, good-humoured face. 'Then you must be Mr. Cadell, sir,' he said. 'Old Quilter was tellin' me yesterday he'd sold the place to a Mr. Cadell.'

'Quite right,' agreed the big man.

'Nice piece of property you've got, sir, if you'll excuse me sayin' so,' ventured the short-sighted little man. 'White Cottage was built in the days when they knew 'ow to build — '

He broke off abruptly as the door was flung suddenly open, and out of the frosty night staggered a skinny undersized man gasping painfully, his drawn face white and shining with perspiration.

''Allo, Yates! What's up?' exclaimed Scowby as the newcomer clutched the back of a chair and tried to recover his breath. 'You been seein' ghosts, too?'

'It's — it's — George 'Icklin' . . . 'Yates

pressed a hand to his heaving chest. ''E's dead!' he panted. 'I found 'im — by the stile, in 'Allows Field — blood all over . . . ' He stopped, unable to continue.

'Give him some brandy!' ordered Cadell sharply.

Mr. Ketler hastened to obey. A glass of the spirit was passed from hand to hand, and Yates gulped its contents eagerly.

'George Hickling — dead!' muttered Mr. Bragg, white-faced. 'Now p'r'aps you'll believe 'e saw the 'Untsman last night!'

A hush followed his words, broken by Cadell: 'Don't you think we'd better do something? The man may not be dead. Where's Hallows Field?'

'The place is about a mile away,' said Ketler. 'There's a footpath — '

'You know the way, Bragg?' interrupted Cadell impatiently. 'Come and show me.' He went over to the door, and Mr. Bragg reluctantly followed him, accompanied by the little man in glasses, and Scowby.

The night was cold, and their footsteps rang on the frozen surface of the road as they strode along. 'This way, sir,' said Mr. Bragg a little tremulously, halting at a gate set in a straggling hedge. 'We follow this footpath across Long Meadow.'

'You lead the way,' said Cadell curtly. Mr. Bragg pushed open the gate, and the others followed him through and along the narrow track that bisected a wide stretch of grazing land. The moon, shining blearily through a film of cloud, shed a diffused light that enabled them to see dimly, and they hurried forward in silence.

Presently they came to a second gate, crossed a rutted lane, and proceeded along another footpath that faced the one they had just traversed. At length Mr. Bragg slowed and turned his head.

'That's the place Yates was talkin' about, sir.' He pointed ahead to the vague outline of a stile.

Cadell was the first to reach the barrier, and swung himself over into the narrow road on the other side. Two yards from the stile he saw a huddled figure on the ground, its dreadful head resting in a pool of crimson, its twisted face a mask of agony and terror.

'It's George, right enough!' muttered

Mr. Bragg, staring down fearfully. "'E must've met with an accident.'

'It was no accident!' said Cadell. 'His head's been battered to pieces!'

He stopped abruptly, the muscles of his face rigid. From somewhere far away, borne faintly on the still, cold air, came the lilt of a familiar melody:

'D'ye ken John Peel with his coat so
   gay,
He lived at Troutbeck once on a day,
But now he's gone, far, far away,
We shall ne'er hear his horn in the
   morning.'

The voice of the singer faded to silence, and Mr. Bragg turned a scared face at his startled companions.

'My gaw', did you 'ear that?' he muttered, his voice husky with fear. 'The 'Untsman!'

2

The Man who Believed in Ghosts

Sir Eustace Chalebury stood at one of the long windows of his library and gazed moodily out across the vista of lawns and gardens to the wooded hillside beyond. A stocky man with thin greying hair and cold blue eyes, he looked more than his fifty-eight years. There was a yellow tinge beneath the ruddy complexion and a looseness at the corners of the full-lipped mouth that spoke eloquently of overindulgence in the grosser appetites — further born out by the unhealthy pouches beneath the dull eyes.

The long, lofty room was a handsome one, lined with bookshelves and panelled in oak that had been ancient when the present owner's great-grandfather had played as a child in the park; for Chalebury Court, with its two hundred and forty acres, had seen many centuries pass, both tranquil and troublesome. A stately house of age-mellowed brick, the original hard lines of which time had mercifully softened with a veil of ivy, it was sited two miles from the village and approached by an avenue of venerable beeches. This drive, known as the Long Walk, was guarded at its entrance below the narrow high street, by wrought-iron gates set between crumbling pillars, which bore on their summit the Chalebury Falcon, part of the family's coat of arms.

Here generations of Chaleburys had lived and loved, hated, and died. A proud family whose motto, carved in worn lettering over the portico of the great main door, truthfully epitomised their attitude to the world: 'Ours is the Ryte.'

The door of the library opened softly, and a black-garbed butler glided into the room. 'Excuse me, Sir Eustace — '

The man at the window turned abruptly from his gloomy contemplation. 'What is it, Foss?'

'Major Hankin would like to see you, sir,' answered the white-haired servant.

Sir Eustace clicked his teeth impatiently, and walked over to the fire. 'Hankin, eh?' he frowned. 'I suppose I'd better see him.

Show him up here. Devilish nuisance!' As the servant moved to open the door, he added: 'Oh, Foss, I — '

'Yes, sir?'

'Have you heard any more gossip in the village?'

Foss hesitated.

'Speak out, man!' snapped Sir Eustace irritably.

'Well, sir,' the butler spoke reluctantly, 'they're all saying that Hickling died because he saw the Huntsman.'

'Nonsense!' Sir Eustace made an angry gesture, but his colour was less pronounced. 'Twaddle! Do these people seriously believe in ghosts?'

'It seems to be the general opinion amongst the villagers, sir,' said Foss deprecatingly.

'The Huntsman! Good gad, are they all mad?' stormed Sir Eustace, the veins of his temple swelling dangerously. 'Just because an ignorant, drunken lout said he saw something — Bah!' He controlled himself with difficulty. 'All right. Bring Major Hankin up.'

The butler went silently out, and his master, still muttering to himself, stood with his back to the fire. In spite of his scepticism concerning the village gossip, he believed in the existence of the Huntsman as wholeheartedly as he disclaimed its possibility. For the legend was to him a tangible thing that brought the fear of death to his heart.

He was standing with his hands behind his back, warming himself at the fire, when Foss ushered in the visitor. Major Hankin, the chief constable for the county, was a thin, red-faced man with ginger hair and an aggressive, bristling moustache. He brought with him a breath of the parade ground, and would have looked more suitably dressed in a uniform than in the quiet tweeds he was wearing.

''Morning, Chalebury!' he greeted in his husky bark. 'Sorry to trouble you, but I suppose you've heard about what happened last night?'

'Of course I've heard of it!' Sir Eustace grunted. 'It's the talk of the village. But I don't see what it's got to do with me.'

'The fellow was one of your gardeners,' answered Hankin. 'Thought perhaps you could help us?'

15

'Well, I can't!' retorted the baronet ungraciously. 'D'you think I know all the private business of my employees? The man was a drunken rascal. Probably got killed in a quarrel with one of his disreputable companions.'

The chief constable shook his head. 'We've been into all that. There's no evidence of any quarrel, and the fellow was popular, with no enemies.'

'Well, I can't help you! Damn it, Hankin, why bother me about it?' Sir Eustace crossed over to the big writing-table and helped himself to a cigar from a large box. Biting the end off irritably, he lit it and blew out a cloud of fragrant smoke. 'Help yourself!' he muttered.

'No, thanks, not just now,' said the major a little stiffly. 'You know what they're saying in the village, of course?'

'You're not seriously taking any notice of that ghost nonsense, are you?'

'I don't believe in ghosts,' retorted the major curtly. 'But there's no doubt this man Hickling saw *something*. Several people assert they've seen someone dressed as a huntsman riding a black horse at night!'

'Rubbish!' snapped the other rudely. But the stubby hand that was holding the cigar trembled slightly, and the heavy face had gone sallower.

'Possibly; but the man who made the discovery with Bragg and Scowby is of a different calibre. He swears he heard somebody singing the last verse of 'John Peel' just after they'd found the body.'

'Perhaps it was the burglar who's been so active in the district lately, celebrating a good haul,' Sir Eustace retorted. 'Instead of chasing ghosts, Hankin, you'd better go after him.'

The chief constable flushed. His fruitless efforts to catch the man to whom the baronet referred was a sore point.

'Four burglaries in two months, and nothing done!' grunted Sir Eustace. 'Why don't you call in Scotland Yard?'

'I and my men are quite capable of dealing with the matter — '

'It looks like it, doesn't it?' sneered the baronet. 'I tell you, Hankin, that if this feller pays a visit to the court, I shall insist on Scotland Yard being called in.'

The chief constable's lips compressed.

'That is rather a matter for me to decide, Chalebury. However, the occasion has not arisen yet, so it's merely a waste of time to argue about it.'

'Well, you'd better see that it doesn't!' snapped Sir Eustace. 'As to this feller Hickling, I know nothing about him except that he was a darn bad gardener.'

Major Hankin took his departure, reflecting that something had upset Chalebury's liver. Passing the post office, he saw a woman come out, and slowed his car. 'Good morning, Miss Renton!' he greeted, bringing the car to a stop beside her. 'Can I give you a lift? I'm passing your house, if you're headed home — '

'I am, as a matter of fact,' she answered. 'It's very nice of you, Major Hankin, but I'd rather walk. I've got a slight headache, and I think the air will do it good.'

She waved a farewell, and he drove on. There was tragedy there, he thought as he turned the car skilfully round a sharp bend in the narrow high street. A year ago Audrey Renton's father had died abroad, and she had not yet recovered from the shock. Unsurprising, considering what great friends she and her father had been. Hankin had known him well: a tall bronzed man with the wanderlust firmly implanted in his system. There was scarcely an unknown part of the world that Andrew Renton had not explored, and this adventurous streak had brought about his death. He had died of fever in some out-of-the-way part of Africa.

For weeks after the news had come through, Audrey had remained shut up in the big house on the hillside, refusing to see anyone except old Dr. Prowse and Willoughby, the elderly servant who had been with the Rentons since her father's childhood. She was young and pretty, and she ought to have been mixing with people of her own age instead of shutting herself up in that gloomy house with only an old woman of nearly seventy for company. It was beginning to tell on her health. Her face was pale and drawn, and that headache she had mentioned . . .

Major Hankin brought his car to a halt outside the tiny rural-looking police station, and dismissed Audrey Renton from his mind.

Inspector Gowper, a broad-shouldered beefy-looking man, was standing in the small charge-room talking to the sergeant when he came in. 'Well, sir,' he said, turning his eyes on the chief constable, 'was Sir Eustace able to suggest anything?'

Hankin shook his head.

'I didn't think he would be. Naturally, a gentleman like him wouldn't know anything about one of 'is gardeners. Hickling's death's a fair mystery, sir. There's nobody local as 'ud want to do him any 'arm, an' there hasn't been no strangers seen.' He hesitated, and then, a little diffidently, continued: 'I s'pose, sir, that this feller Mr. Cadell couldn't 'ave 'ad anything to do with it? He's the only stranger — '

'Of course he couldn't!' broke in Major Hankin impatiently. 'He's a very well-known, famous author. What possible reason could he have for killing a man like Hickling?'

'I couldn't tell yer that, sir,' replied Gowper. 'What reason could anybody 'ave 'ad?'

'Yes, it's an extraordinary business.'

'Yes, sir. An' the most extr'ordin'ry thing about it is the 'Untsman.'

'May be some truth in that story,'

muttered Hankin doubtfully. 'Mr. Cadell says he heard somebody singing a verse of 'John Peel', but it might've been one of the villagers going home.'

'It's been seen, too, sir,' Gowper reminded him. 'Two or three people swear they've both seen an' heard it — or *something*. An' Hickling's supposed to 'ave seen it the night before 'e was killed.'

'I know — I know!' said Major Hankin. 'But if anything of the kind has been seen, then somebody's playing a joke. What line of investigation are you adopting now?'

Gowper told him. It was practically only the usual routine inquiries, but the chief constable could suggest nothing better. He took his leave soon after, vaguely troubled in his mind at the unsatisfactory progress that was being made.

He was to be even more troubled before the next day dawned, for during the night Chalebury Court was broken into, a quantity of gold plate and valuable sporting trophies stolen, and the only clue to the robber was a piece of newspaper smeared with thick glue and the tattered remains of a woollen stocking.

3

Stocking-foot

Mr. Budd came ponderously along the corridor and tapped at the door of the assistant commissioner's room. A muffled voice snapped a curt, 'Come in!' Colonel Blair raised a sleek grey head and greeted him across his huge, untidy desk. 'Sit down, Superintendent,' he said, nodding towards a chair in front of him. 'I'm sending you into the country.'

The stout man squeezed his large bulk into the chair with difficulty and waited, his sleepy eyes half-closed.

'You remember that epidemic of robberies in Hampshire last year?' went on the assistant commissioner.

Mr. Budd nodded. He was not likely to forget them easily, for it was one of the few occasions on which he had not shown to advantage. 'Stockin'-foot, sir,' he said.

'That's the fellow! He broke into a

dozen houses in less than three months, and was never caught. You fell down badly on that.'

The stout superintendent coloured but said nothing. He had been severely reprimanded at the time for his failure, and the memory still rankled.

'I'm giving you a chance to retrieve your reputation,' continued the assistant commissioner. 'The chief constable of Southshire has asked for our assistance in connection with a number of burglaries that have taken place recently in the district, and it looks to me as if this same fellow is operating again.'

'What's your reasoning, sir?' asked Mr. Budd.

'The modus operandi is similar. In every instance, access was gained to the burgled house by means of a ground-floor window from which a portion of the glass had been cut out near the catch. To prevent the glass that was removed from dropping, a piece of newspaper smeared with thick glue was used.'

'That sounds like Stockin'-foot. He used the same means in Hampshire.'

'A more important reason is that in two cases, portions of a woollen stocking were discovered on the scene of the robbery, and that was one of the characteristics of the Hampshire burglaries last year.'

'It certainly looks as if it were the same fellow,' murmured Mr. Budd sleepily.

'I'm sure of it. And since the Southshire police have asked for assistance, I'm sending you along. But you've got to make good this time.'

'I'll do my best, sir.'

'You've got to do more than that!' snapped Colonel Blair a little unreasonably. 'You've got to find this clever robber, and I'm warning you I shan't accept any excuses for failure.' He flicked open some typewritten sheets in a folder on his blotting pad, found the one he sought, and frowned at it. 'The latest robbery,' he said, 'the last of a series of five during the past ten weeks, occurred the night before last. Sir Eustace Chalebury's house, Chalebury Court, was broken into, and a considerable amount of gold plate and sporting trophies was stolen. I know Chalebury, and if I'm not very much mistaken, it was he who insisted that the local people should call in the Yard.'

'Chalebury,' murmured Mr. Budd. 'Wasn't there a murder at a place called Chalebury a few nights ago?'

The assistant commissioner nodded. 'Yes. A fellow called George Hickling was bludgeoned to death. There was some talk of a ghost being responsible.' He made an impatient gesture. 'I don't suppose it's got anything to do with this affair, though. There's been nothing in his previous exploits to suggest that this fellow, Stocking-foot, is a killer. However, if there is any connection it's up to you to find it.' His tone conveyed that the interview was ended.

The melancholy Sergeant Leek looked up when the stout superintendent returned to his own cheerless office. 'What did old Blair want?' he asked

'It's usual to refer to him as Colonel Blair,' said his superior admonishingly. 'Remember that! And officers with the rank of superintendent like to be addressed as 'sir' occasionally, too!'

The lanky sergeant sighed.

'You'd better start gettin' the habit,' went on Mr. Budd, 'because we're goin' to the huntin', shootin' and fishin' district, where they're great sticklers for respect — s'long as it comes from the other feller.'

'We are?' said the startled Leek. 'When?'

'Just as soon as we can pack a bag and catch the train.'

'What for?'

'To chase foxes!' snarled his companion irritably. 'Don't ask so many questions. Find out when the next train leaves for Chalebury, and be ready to catch it.'

The next train left in an hour and a half, and Mr. Budd arranged to meet the lugubrious Leek at the station. There was no sign of the lean sergeant when he arrived on the platform, and he was looking about for him when a cheery voice called his name. He turned to look with disfavour at the pleasant-faced man who was approaching him with a broad grin.

'Hello!' cried this individual boisterously. 'What are you doing here? Preparing to visit the ancestral home for the weekend?'

'No,' snapped Mr. Budd.

Tommy Weston, crime reporter on the *Morning Wire*, took his arm affectionately. 'Are you travelling by this train?'

'Supposin' I am, what's it got to do with you?' grunted Mr. Budd offensively.

'That means you are! That's fine — so am I. My news editor's come all over psychic. He thinks a good ghost story will send up the circulation of the paper. The Huntsman of Chalebury was, at one time, the most famous ghost in England — and he's appeared again.'

The stout man sniffed scornfully. 'Ghosts! You make me tired.'

'You were born tired,' said Tommy cheerfully. 'You ought to take more exercise, Budd.'

'There's my sergeant,' said Mr. Budd, waving towards the disconsolate figure who had drifted through the barrier, grasping a dilapidated suitcase. 'Must attract his attention, or he'll go gettin' into the wrong train.'

The lean sergeant saw the signal and came shambling towards them. 'Sorry I'm late,' he apologised mournfully, 'but I couldn't find me spurs — '

'Your *what*?'

'You said somethin' about 'untin' — '

'I also mentioned shootin' and fishin',' broke in the superintendent. 'Have you brought a gun and a rod as well?'

'I ain't got neither of those,' Leek answered regretfully, 'but I 'ad some spurs belongin' to me uncle, and — '

His explanation was drowned by Tommy's hoot of laughter. 'Can you see him?' he chuckled. 'Tally-ho, yoicks, and all the rest of it.'

'Well, I thought they might come in useful,' said the injured Leek.

'Were you under the impression we were goin' to chase Stockin'-foot on 'orseback?' said Mr. Budd sarcastically.

Tommy whistled. 'So that's who you're after, is it? If nothing comes of my ghost trip, I may get a story after all.'

'You'll get nothing!' growled the superintendent. 'Come on — if we don't hurry up, the train'll go without us.'

They found an empty compartment, and had just settled themselves when the guard's whistle sounded and the train began to move. Mr. Budd ensconced himself in a corner and slept — or pretended to sleep — for the greater part of the journey. Tommy Weston, glancing at him now and again over the top of the magazine he was reading, marvelled, and not for the first time, at the difference between this portly man's outward appearance and the brain behind the placid, rather bovine face.

He remained oblivious to his surroundings until the train slid gently along the platform at their destination. Then he opened his eyes wearily, yawned, and rose heavily to his feet. 'I wonder if those cock-eyed county people have sent anyone to meet us,' he said.

The 'cock-eyed county people' had. A stocky, red-faced man waiting near the ticket barrier came forward as they passed through. 'Sup'ntendent Budd?' he inquired, and, when the big man nodded: 'I'm Inspector Gowper, sir. Major 'Ankin, the chief constable, asked me to meet you. I've got a car outside.'

He led the way to the exit, and as they

followed, Tommy took the stout man's arm affectionately. 'I suppose I can have a lift to Chalebury?' he murmured.

'I s'pose you can do nothin' of the sort!' retorted Mr. Budd. 'You're not in this, Weston. We've got nothin' to do with ghosts.'

He shook off the reporter's hand and ambled over to the car, where Gowper was waiting. Climbing with difficulty into the back of the shabby police car, he watched the porter sleepily while he stowed away their luggage, handed him a tip, and settled back comfortably, with the lean sergeant wedged in beside him.

The distance to the village was a little over twenty miles. It took just under an hour to do the journey in Inspector Gowper's ancient car, and dusk was falling by the time they drew up in front of the tiny station-house.

Major Hankin was waiting for them in the charge room, standing in front of the cheerful fire. 'I've taken rooms for yourself and your sergeant at the Fox and Hounds, Superintendent,' he said when the preliminary greetings were over. 'Inspector Gowper will take you along as soon as we've finished with our business.'

The business did not take very long. Mr. Budd was provided with a list of the houses Stocking-foot had favoured with his attentions, and Gowper produced such meagre clues as that enterprising burglar had left behind. These consisted of some scraps of torn woollen stocking and one or two pieces of glue-smeared newspaper.

'The latest robbery was at Chalebury Court the night before last,' said the chief constable. 'The house was entered by means of the pantry window, and the usual method was adopted of cutting out a small pane of glass near the hasp. We found the glass, with the glued newspaper adhering to it, on the path outside. We've had it tested for fingerprints, but there were none.'

'There wouldn't be with Stockin'-foot, sir,' said Mr. Budd. 'He doesn't make mistakes like that.'

'I understand you've had some experience of his methods before?'

'I have, sir!' agreed the big man feelingly. 'I was after 'im last year when 'e did that series in Hampshire, but I couldn't catch 'im then.'

'Well, I hope you'll have better luck this time. I may say that Sir Eustace Chalebury is putting a great deal of faith in you. He's under the impression, I'm afraid, that we on our own are not, er, capable of dealing with this clever robber.' There was an undertone of annoyance in his voice. 'Sir Eustace will want to see you. Will you go up to the court tonight, or leave it until tomorrow?'

'I think I'd rather leave it till tomorrow. Ternight I'd like to settle down an' get me bearings, so ter speak.'

'Very well,' Major Hankin said with a nod. 'I won't interfere with your methods of investigation, Superintendent. I believe in letting a man who knows his job do it in his own way. Every bit of help we can give you is, of course, at your disposal. Now, I expect you'd like to have a wash and some food after your journey. Gowper will take you to the inn.'

Mr. Ketler greeted his guests with respectful interest. 'Very glad to 'ave you 'ere, gen'l'men,' he said. 'An' I 'opes you'll catch this burglar feller. Wot with robberies an' murder an' ghosts, the village is in a proper scare, I can tell yer.'

'Ah, yes,' murmured Mr. Budd. 'There was a murder, wasn't there?'

The landlord became voluble. With great gusto he related what had happened to George Hickling, and what had foreshadowed the tragedy. 'Not that I'm a believer in ghosts an' suchlike things meself,' he concluded. 'But there's no doubt that somethin' is abroad at nights. I was only sayin' ter the newspaper gen'l'man — '

'What newspaper gentleman?' demanded Mr. Budd, and he was answered by a cheery voice from the open door of the bar-parlour.

'Me!' it said. 'The original gentleman from Fleet Street!'

'Oh, *you're* here, are you,' grunted Mr. Budd.

Tommy Weston looked up with a grin from a food-laden table. 'Come and join me! Beer, cold beef, pickles, and jam tart. Pull up a chair and fortify the inner man!'

Mr. Budd became suddenly aware that he was hungry. 'Are you stayin' here?' he asked, entering the little cosily furnished room.

'I am,' answered the reporter. 'I've got the room next to yours. Always make your headquarters at a pub, that's my motto.'

'Well, I s'pose it can't be helped,' said Mr. Budd resignedly.

The beaming Mr. Ketler brought more food, and Leek and Mr. Budd joined the reporter in a hearty meal. When it was over, they went into the tap-room. Mr. Bragg, Scowby, Perkins and Yates, together with the usual habitués of the Fox and Hounds, were gathered before the bar, talking earnestly. They stopped and stared at the trio as they made their way to a secluded corner, and there was much whispering. After a little while, however, the conversation was resumed. It consisted entirely of a discussion about the murder of Hickling, the Huntsman, and the robbery at Chalebury Court, Mr. Budd listening with interest.

'A very instructive evenin'!' was his comment when Mr. Ketler had got rid of the last of his customers and shut up for the night.

'Very,' agreed Tommy Weston. 'Nothing like soaking yourself in local gossip. You learn more that way than you would by a thousand questions. What do you say to a walk before turning in?'

It was a clear, cold, frosty night with a brilliant moon, and they set off briskly down the narrow road bordered with black-thorn hedges, beyond which stretched the undulating country. The air was sharp and invigorating after the smoke-laden atmosphere of the tap-room. At last Mr. Budd stopped.

'I think we'd better be turnin' back now,' he said. 'I'm beginnin' ter — Listen! Am I dreamin', or can you hear it too?'

'I can hear somebody singin',' said Leek.

'Quiet!' snapped the big man; and in the silence they heard the old melody come clearly across the wide expanse of open country:

'*D'ye ken John Peel, with his coat so gay,*
He lived at Troutbeck once on a day,
But now he's gone, far, far away —'

'There he is!' cried Tommy Weston. 'Look! Over there, by that belt of trees!'

And, looking, they saw. The black horse showed clearly; the moonlight caught the pink of the rider's coat. And then horse and rider disappeared over the ridge of the hill, and only the words of the song came floating faintly to their ears.

4

The Inquest

Mr. Budd woke early on the following morning, and hoisting himself out of bed, surveyed the weather from the latticed window of his bedroom without enthusiasm. The hard frost of the previous night had held. The little garden of the inn, the roadway beyond, and such of the countryside as came within his vision was covered in rime.

While he washed and dressed, he speculated on what he had seen and heard the night before. There was some truth, then, in the village gossip concerning the Huntsman. He had seen the black horse, and its pink-coated rider — seen it and heard the faint, plaintive lilt of that ancient melody. The question was, did this supposedly phantom huntsman have any connection with the business that had brought him to Chalebury? The Huntsman was no concern of his unless he had a bearing on the elusive Stocking-foot. What he had heard and seen in company with Tommy Weston and Leek was undoubtedly human. His phlegmatic nature refused to countenance the existence of ghosts.

If the Huntsman was just a practical joker out to scare the simple-minded and superstitious people of Chalebury, he could continue to gallop about the countryside, singing his song, until he was tired. But there might be another explanation. Anybody abroad at night, on business that was better not inquired into too closely, could have adopted no more useful disguise, since few would investigate what they believed to be of supernatural origin. And this might be very useful indeed — to Stocking-foot, for example.

Mr. Budd went down to the bar-parlour still pondering the matter. A cheerful fire was blazing merrily in the grate, and a pretty, rosy-cheeked young woman was laying the table for breakfast.

'Good mornin', my dear!' said the big man, warming his hands. 'I s'pose you'd call this seasonable weather, eh?'

'Yes, sir,' said the woman, her face

dimpling into a smile.

'Well, I won't tell you what *I* call it,' grunted Mr. Budd. 'It wouldn't be fit for a young lady like you to hear! Still, I s'pose it's good for huntin', eh?'

'Oh, yes, sir,' replied the woman. 'The Chalebury are meetin' tomorrer up at the court. Do you 'unt, sir?'

'I s'pose I do, in a manner of speakin',' murmured Mr. Budd. 'But it's somethin' more dangerous than foxes.'

The woman had finished setting the table, but she lingered. 'You're a detective, ain't yer, sir?' she asked, plucking at a corner of her apron nervously. 'I 'eard tell there was a detective come from Lunnon.' She looked as if she was about to say more, but remained silent.

Mr. Budd regarded her kindly. 'Now, don't be nervous. I'm not a very formidable feller. You was goin' ter tell me somethin', an' then you thought better of it, isn't that right?'

She was screwing her apron up with both hands now. 'I don't want ter tell yer nuthin', I don't reely.' She paused, and passed the tip of her tongue over her red lips. 'I s'pose you'll be goin' ter the inquest this mornin', won't yer?'

'Is it this mornin'?' The stout superintendent guessed that she was referring to the inquiry into the death of George Hickling, although he had not known it was to take place that day.

'Of course it is, sir,' she replied a little scornfully. 'You know it is. Ain't that what yer 'ere for?'

Mr. Budd could have truthfully answered 'no' to this question, since he had not come to Chalebury to find the killer of George Hickling, unless he happened also to be Stocking-foot; but he thought it wiser not to say so. This buxom country woman was trying to make up her mind to tell him something — something that she either knew, or thought she knew, that was worrying her.

'Well, maybe I shall look in,' he said. 'Did you know this feller, Hicklin'?'

'Yes, sir. Everybody knew 'im round these parts,' she said, nodding, and trying to smooth out the creases she had put into the ill-treated apron. 'I didn't know 'im any better than nobody else, but — '

She broke off, hesitated, and then: 'I'll 'ave ter go an' see about the breakfasts.' She almost ran from the room.

'Now what was she goin' ter say?' Mr. Budd muttered. 'Hm! That woman 'ull be worth cultivatin'. She knows somethin'.'

At that moment Tommy Weston came breezing into the room. 'Hello!' he greeted cheerily. 'The first up, eh? What have you been doing to our fair Abigail, you old rascal?'

'To who?' grunted Mr. Budd.

'Our lovely serving wench — the pride of Chalebury,' explained Tommy. 'She nearly knocked me over as she came flying out of this room, covered in maidenly confusion, to escape from your evil designs — '

'Don't be a bigger fool than Nature made you!' broke in the big man irritably. 'Is my sergeant up?'

'So far as I know, he's sleeping the sleep that a clear conscience inspires,' replied the reporter. 'As I dressed I could hear him through the wall. It was like a man with adenoids swallowing his bath-water.'

At that moment Mr. Ketler came in. 'Good morning, gen'l'men!' said that genial man. 'I 'ope you slept quite comfortable?'

'Too comfortable for my sergeant, apparently,' said Mr. Budd. 'I think I'd better go an' wake 'im. If somebody don't, he won't get up at all!'

When he came back the landlord had gone, and Tommy was alone.

'They're holding the inquest on Hickling this morning,' said the reporter. 'In the school-room, at ten o'clock. Are you going? Ketler says that everybody is.'

'Then I must be,' said the big man, who had already made up his mind to attend the inquiry for this very reason. 'I s'pose you'll be there?'

'You bet your life I shall!' answered Tommy promptly. 'There's a big story here somewhere,' he went on seriously. 'I can sense it. This village is going to be front-page news before very long.'

His prophecy was fulfilled sooner than either of them expected, for the combined forces Fate had marshalled, which were to make Chalebury world-notorious, were even at that moment working up towards the startling and unexpected climax.

When Mr. Budd and his companions reached the small red-brick building that normally housed the infant population of Chalebury, they found a massed crowd of people both within and without. The circumstances surrounding the death of Hickling and the gossip concerning the Huntsman had aroused an intense curiosity that had spread to the many large houses in the district, so that there was a goodly sprinkling of the 'County'. They stood about in groups, loud-voiced and aloof.

The big man caught sight of Major Hankin among the throng and went over to speak to him. 'Good morning, Superintendent,' said the chief constable. 'I'm glad you're here. Gowper will find you a place inside. I don't expect the proceedings to take very long. We've no evidence to offer except that of identification and the cause of death, and we shall ask for an adjournment. I doubt if you'll be very interested, but it will give you an opportunity to see most of the people in the neighbourhood.'

'That's what I thought, sir,' said Mr. Budd, suppressing a yawn. 'And, of course, there's always the possibility that this murder may be mixed up with Stockin'-foot.'

'Yes, there's the possibility of that,' Hankin agreed, 'though I can't see what motive he could have had for killing a feller like Hickling.'

'No more can I, sir. An' I'm not sayin' he did. I'm only lookin' for somethin' that'll give me a line to 'im. We can't even be certain that 'e's operatin' from the district, or that he'll do another job in these parts.'

'I appreciate that, and I fully realise the difficulty of your task. I suppose you've heard of our ghost scare?'

'I've not only 'eard of it, I've seen it!'

'You've seen the Huntsman? When?'

'Last night, sir.' Mr. Budd told the chief constable what he and the others had witnessed.

'Extraordinary!' Hankin muttered. 'You're the sixth person who's seen and heard this — this horseman abroad at night. Your description tallies with the others. A big black horse and the rider dressed in a pink coat — in fact, the Huntsman of the legend.' He paused and pursed his lips. 'D'you suppose it could be a trick of this feller, Stocking-foot? Maybe it'd be worth-while trying to trap this feller, whoever he is.'

To Hankin's surprise, Mr. Budd showed no enthusiasm at the suggestion. 'We couldn't accuse him of being Stockin'-foot, because we don't know what Stockin'-foot looks like. He'd only have to say 'e was doin' this ghost business for a joke, an' we couldn't do anything. There's no law against ridin' about the country at night. No, I don't think we want to trap him, but I'd like to get a good look at him! Who's that feller over there, sir?'

The chief constable turned and followed the direction of his eyes. 'That's Mr. Henry Cadell, the novelist. He's a newcomer to the district. In fact, it was he who found the body of Hickling.'

'Hm! Fine-lookin' man, ain't he?' murmured the stout superintendent, surveying the huge broad-shouldered figure with interest. 'Now where 'ave I seen 'im before?'

45

'I expect you've seen his photograph in the papers.'

'Maybe that was it, sir,' agreed Mr. Budd, his sleepy eyes still fixed on the novelist; but he knew that it wasn't a photograph that had set that elusive memory working. Somewhere, in circumstances that he could not recall, he had seen Henry Cadell in the flesh, and the occasion was associated in his mind with something unpleasant.

His attention was distracted from Cadell by a harsh voice behind him. 'Mornin', Hankin,' it snapped irritably. 'What the devil d'you mean by gettin' me subpoenaed to this damn poppy-show, eh?'

Mr. Budd turned and saw that the speaker was a man with dull eyes and an unhealthy complexion. 'Really, Chalebury,' said the chief constable angrily, his face reddening, 'I wish you'd moderate your language. You were subpoenaed because, in the opinion of the coroner, your evidence was necessary to this inquiry — '

'Rubbish!' interrupted Sir Eustace rudely. 'I told you I know nothing about

Hicklin', an' don't want to know anything about him!' He stared at Mr. Budd curiously. 'Who's this?' he demanded curtly.

Major Hankin introduced them.

'Oh, so you're the feller from Scotland Yard, are you?' grunted Chalebury. 'Well, I hope you'll make a better job of catching this burglar than our own people did. Why haven't you been up to the court? That's where the robbery happened, not here!'

'So I understand, sir,' said Mr. Budd in his slowest drawl. 'Do you think, then, that I shall find the burglar at Chalebury Court?'

'Eh?' The baronet frowned. 'Of course not!'

'Then it's not much good me goin' there, is it, sir? You see, I want ter find out where he is, not where he was.'

Sir Eustace's fish-like eyes met the sleepy brown ones with a slightly puzzled expression, and Major Hankin coughed. 'I think, Chalebury,' he said hastily, 'that it'd be better if the superintendent was left to work in his own way.'

'I don't give a damn how he works,' snapped Sir Eustace, 'so long as he gets my property back.' He turned away and went to speak to a group of men and women who were talking loudly a short distance away.

'It's time we went inside,' said Hankin, glancing at his watch. 'Come along, and I'll find Gowper.'

'An' that's the 'County',' muttered Mr. Budd to the silent and melancholy Leek as they followed the chief constable into the building. 'The 'untin', shootin' an' fishin' crowd what thinks the world was made to amuse 'em. My lord, look at 'em! What a bunch! Why, they can't even chase a fox without a lot o' dogs to 'elp 'em!'

Inspector Gowper was talking to the coroner, a dapper bald man, when they entered the crowded little room. He came over after a word with Major Hankin and found them seats near the coroner's table, and while the jury were being sworn Mr. Budd gazed leisurely about him.

Tommy Weston had managed to squeeze into a good position, and was whispering to three other men whom Mr.

Budd guessed were also newspaper-men. Mr. Bragg and Mr. Scowby, looking rather self-conscious and important in their Sunday best, were seated on the bench reserved for the witnesses, talking in whispers to the nervous-looking Yates.

A short distance away from them sat an old man with a thin, lined face and snow-white hair that was brushed back from a high forehead. The face was kindly in spite of the firm lips and stubborn chin, and curiously sensitive. The big man wondered who this distinguished old gentleman might be, and learned later that he was Dr. Prowse, the police surgeon for the district.

Among the numerous faces waiting expectantly for the proceedings to begin were many that interested Mr. Budd. Rather amusedly he wondered whether Stocking-foot was present. If he was responsible for the murder of Hickling, then it was quite possible he might have come to hear the result of the inquest. It struck the superintendent that it would be worthwhile to find out from Gowper if any strangers were present.

The jury came back from viewing the body, and the coroner opened the proceedings. From the point of view of the many people who had come in the hope of hearing something sensational, they were disappointingly brief.

Sir Eustace Chalebury identified the dead man as having been one of his under-gardeners, and Henry Cadell, Mr. Bragg, Scowby and the nervous Yates gave a brief account of the circumstances in which the body had been discovered. There was a little stir of interest at the mention of the Huntsman; but when the subject was not taken up by the coroner, this died. When Dr. Prowse had supplied a highly technical description of the cause of death, Inspector Gowper asked for an adjournment. This was granted, and the short proceedings came to an end.

'Nothing very sensational about that!' remarked Tommy Weston as he found himself next to Mr. Budd in the crush at the exit.

'What did you expect?' growled the stout man. 'Someone to shoot the coroner?'

'It would've made a fine story — '

Tommy broke off suddenly and gripped the other's arm. 'Who's that?' he demanded. 'D'you know her?'

Mr. Budd looked across at the slim figure in the neat tweed costume that had attracted the reporter's attention. 'No,' he replied. 'You keep your mind on yer business, an' don't go messin' around after gals.'

'She's lovely!' breathed Tommy, gazing after her. 'But there's something wrong somewhere. Did you ever see such a sad expression on anyone's face before? I'll bet there's a story there.'

Mr. Budd snorted disparagingly. He had no foreknowledge of the part Audrey Renton was to play in the events that were to come, nor any inkling of the dreadful secret she was so jealously guarding.

5

Mr. Budd Collects Facts

More because it seemed to be expected of him than because he hoped to learn anything of importance, Mr. Budd went up to Chalebury Court to inspect the scene of Stocking-foot's latest exploit. He was shown the pantry window with its neat round hole, and the cases in the great hall from which the plate and trophies had been taken. The locks of these had been skilfully picked. He examined the ground beneath the window, but there were no marks that were at all helpful, and he had not expected to find any.

An interview with the servants resulted in no addition to his scanty supply of knowledge. None of them had heard anything during the night, and the robbery had not been discovered until Foss, the butler, had come down in the morning. Neither could the rest of the household offer any useful information.

Lady Chalebury, a thin woman with a face that reminded Mr. Budd of a once-famous horse, thought she had heard a sound like the gentle closing of a door; but she couldn't be sure of this or of the time when she thought she had heard it. Captain Linden and Mrs. Keeling-Kerr, two guests staying in the house, had heard nothing. They gave Mr. Budd the impression that they had passed the whole of their lives hearing nothing, and he left no wiser than when he had come. With the exception of Sir Eustace's son, Arnold Chalebury, who had gone over to inspect some hunters for sale in the neighbouring town, the superintendent had seen everybody who had been at the court on the night of the burglary without learning anything that was likely to help him in his search for the elusive Stocking-foot.

He had not put any great faith in the possibility of finding a clue at Chalebury Court. His pessimism as he walked slowly back to the Fox and Hounds was not so much due to the unfruitfulness of his visit as to the realisation of the difficulty of his task.

He had asked Gowper what strangers there had been at the inquest, and had received the disconcerting reply that with the exception of the pressmen, there had been none. Unless, therefore, Stocking-foot was someone well-known in the district, he had not been present. It was more than probable that at that moment he was seeking fresh fields and pastures new, in which case it was a sheer waste of time remaining in Chalebury, except that it would be almost an equal waste of time to go anywhere else. But the idea of going back to the Yard and again reporting failure was unthinkable, so Chalebury was as good a base of operations as any.

Reaching the inn, Mr. Budd found Sergeant Leek carefully examining his long, lean face in the old-fashioned overmantel. 'What d'yer think you're doin'?' grunted the big man.

The sergeant turned hurriedly, blushing deeply. 'It's a man's duty to try an' look 'is best,' he mumbled. ''Ow did yer get on up at the court?'

The superintendent eyed his subordinate suspiciously. 'Why are you blushing like an overgrown schoolgirl?'

'I ain't blushing!' protested the embarrassed sergeant. 'It — it's the 'eat of the fire.'

'The heat o' me grandmother's stuffed canary!' broke in Mr. Budd. 'You've bin up ter somethin' that you shouldn't 'ave bin.'

He stopped as the door opened, and the woman he had seen at breakfast came in carrying a tray with a glass of yellow liquid. 'Your lime-juice-an'-soda, sir,' she said.

Leek took the glass awkwardly. 'Thank you, Elsie!' he muttered; and for the first time in his life, Mr. Budd saw his long face twist into a sickly smile. It was the most ghastly performance he had ever seen.

'So that's it, is it?' he said, when the woman had gone. 'Elsie, eh? That's the reason for all this film-star stuff in front of the mirror.'

'I called 'er Elsie because that's 'er name,' said the sergeant. 'I asked 'er, an' she told me.' He took a sip from his glass and coughed. 'What's the 'arm in that?'

'None, so long as it remains at that,' answered his superior. 'But with your hot blood an' well-known recklessness, there's no knowin' what may 'appen!'

'I wouldn't do 'er no 'arm,' said the sergeant seriously. 'I like that woman. I took a likin' to 'er direc'y I set eyes on 'er. I 'spose there comes a time to all men when the one woman enters their life . . . Somethin' seems to 'ave come over me.'

'You look as if you were goin' to be sick,' said Mr. Budd unkindly.

'Jest a little cottage with a bit o' garden, an' 'er waitin' fer you after the long day's toil!' murmured the sergeant dreamily.

'If you go on like that, *I* shall be sick!' snarled Mr. Budd, and he went in search of the genial landlord.

Mr. Ketler was in the tap-room, polishing glasses and beaming good-humouredly at his customers. Mr. Budd ordered a pint of beer, and calling the landlord aside, put the question that had been the reason for his seeking him.

Mr. Ketler considered. 'Well, there was Joe Eales,' he replied in a conspiratorial whisper. ''E saw the thing closer than wot anybody 'as. Joe does a bit of poachin', an' the 'Untsman passed within a yard or two o' where 'e was setting 'is snares. An' then there was Dick Jarman — 'e's a keeper up on the estate — 'e seen it one night!' He mentioned two other people who had also either heard or seen the Chalebury ghost, and Mr. Budd wrote down their addresses.

After lunch he set out to interview them in turn. Jarman was the nearest, occupying a small cottage in the great park attached to the estate, and Mr. Budd luckily found him at home. He greeted Mr. Budd pleasantly, and looked interested when he heard the reason for his call.

'Well, yes, sir, I did see somethin',' he said, speaking in the slow, careful manner of the countryman. 'About a week ago it were. I was comin' out o' the 'Ome Covert when I 'eard the thud o' gallopin' hoofs. They was a long way off, over t'other side of the Mound — but I could

57

'ear 'em plain, although I couldn't see nuthin'. In a bit 'e comes over the ridge, an' then I sees 'im — a big black 'orse gallopin' like the wind, an' 'is rider wearin' a huntsman's pink coat an' peak cap. 'E went tearin' across the Long Meadow an' out o' sight be'ind the belt o' trees what marks the beginnin' of Black Wood, an' I 'eard 'im singin' 'John Peel' long arter I couldn't see 'im no more.'

'What sort of a night was it?'

'Cold an' frosty, with a nearly full moon, sir. Pretty nigh the same as it were last night!'

'An' do you believe that what you saw was a ghost?'

'Well, I don't quite know, sir,' Jarman replied slowly. 'I wouldn't like ter say either way. It give me a fair turn at the time, I can tell yer!'

'I s'pose there are plenty of black horses about these parts?'

'Scores on 'em, sir.' The keeper smiled. 'You're thinkin' that maybe somebody's playin' a joke?'

'Or pretendin' to be a ghost for some reason best known to themselves.'

'Maybe you're right, sir,' said Jarman; but his voice lacked conviction.

There was nothing more to be learned from the keeper, and refusing the cup of tea which the hospitable Mrs. Jarman tried to press on him, the superintendent took his departure and went to seek the abode of Joe Eales.

The poacher lived in a tiny wooden house, little more than a shack set in a square of untidy garden, on the outskirts of the village. Again Mr. Budd was lucky and found his man at home, but here his reception was very different. Joe Eales was a little rat of a man, thin-faced and surly, and he evidently viewed Mr. Budd's intrusion into his privacy with suspicion.

'Who said I seen anythin'? An' wot does it matter ter you wot I seen?' he demanded. 'You clear out! I don't want your sort 'angin' round 'ere!'

'Now see here, my man!' Mr. Budd said sternly. 'Except that you can give me some information, I'm not interested in you. You'll either tell me what I want to know, or you'll sleep tonight in a cell! Understand?'

Mr. Eales evidently understood very well, for his truculent manner subsided. 'Wot d'yer want ter know?' he asked sullenly.

'I've told you what I want ter know!' snapped the superintendent. 'You saw this ghost, or whatever it is, an' you saw it at close quarters. Now what did yer see?'

Mr. Eales launched into a reluctant narrative which, shorn of its many deviations and redundancy, whittled down to this:

He had been in the vicinity of Newnham's Spinney late on the night prior to the murder of George Hickling — he offered no explanation for his presence there — when he had heard something moving among the trees. Not wishing to be seen, he had crouched down behind a screen of bushes until whoever was making the sounds had gone. The bushes were on the edge of a kind of glade bathed in bright moonlight, and presently into this patch of radiance from the shadow of the little wood had come an enormous coal-black horse ridden by a man in the pink coat of a huntsman. Horse and rider passed within a couple of yards of the terrified Mr. Eales, and he had seen the face.

'It wasn't 'uman,' he asserted. 'It was awful — all puffed up an' white an' glistening . . . '

'What d'you mean, glistenin'?' demanded Mr. Budd.

'All shiny-like,' replied the little poacher with a shiver. 'I ran like 'ell, an' then I 'eard it singin' . . . '

★　★　★

After he had gone to bed that night, tired with his day's exertions, Mr. Budd thought over what he had gleaned and found it disappointingly little. The other two people who had seen the Huntsman had added nothing to his stock of knowledge concerning that mysterious spook. They had only glimpsed the black horse and its pink-coated rider from a distance. Joe Eales was the nearest to a description — a face 'puffed up and white and glistening'. Probably a disguise. Some kind of mask, no doubt. But he had not come to Chalebury to chase ghosts, real or otherwise. He had come to find a solid, material burglar. And how far had he got with that?

Not very far. Still, he had found one or two oddities. That woman who had wanted to say something and hadn't, and the elusive memory which the sight of Henry Cadell had conjured up. In what circumstances had he met the man before? Something unpleasant. He was still wondering when he fell asleep.

6

The Meet!

It is as difficult to disassociate the sport of fox-hunting from the English countryside as to think of bread without thinking of butter. The Quorn, the Pytchley and the Belvoir are names as familiar as Piccadilly, Charing Cross and St. Paul's Cathedral. And to them must be added the Chalebury. It is one of the oldest hunts, dating from 1772, established by one Sir Peter Chalebury, the father of old Sir Thomas, whose exploits had been the beginning of the Huntsman, and has been mentioned in the writings of Surtees and Bulwer Lytton. From then until the present day, it has taken its place among the first-class packs; and the meet, on the wide gravel sweep in front of the great arched entrance to Chalebury Court, is now, as always, a colourful, picturesque sight.

The pale winter sun floods the scene, causing the hoarfrost on tree and bush and shrub to glisten like powdered glass, bringing out the colour in the coats of the whips and the M.F.H., and making the glossy horses shine with the brilliance of well-polished leather. The hounds, twenty couples, have been brought from the kennels and are waiting, sniffing the air impatiently, while the dignified Foss and three footmen administer stirrup-cup to the forty-odd members of the hunt.

Sir Eustace, sitting easily on his big black mare, is at his best. The troubles and fears that normally beset him are for the moment forgotten, and he is looking forward to a good run. The weather is perfect, and the scent should lie well. His heavy face has lost something of its sallowness in the keen, cold air, and he is almost genial as he leads the hunt to a cover near the house, followed on foot by such of the villagers as have come to witness the start.

'Hark in, hark!' The eager hounds vanish into the gorse, and for some minutes there is a breathless silence. Then a whimper is heard. A hound challenges — then another and another. They have found! In an instant the hunt is streaming across country — two score men and women on as many horses, with twenty couples of hounds — in pursuit of one small, defenceless fox!

Over hedges and ditches — across alternate grass and plough. The fox has made a long point, but the scent is hot and the run looks like being a good one. The field has thinned out, the speed and the jumps proving too much for some of the weaker members. A fair number have, however, kept in line, and among these are Captain Linden and Mrs. Keeling-Kerr. Sir Eustace and the whips are in the van, keeping closely on the heels of the racing hounds, who, with sterns well down, seem determined to outpace the horses behind them. The fox is making for a small wood where there is an old 'earth'. But the gamekeepers have stopped it, and the panting, sweating quarry can find no sanctuary there. He is sighted across one of the 'rides' with which the wood is cut in two directions; sighted again as he breaks cover.

'Gone away!' The cry rings out on the clear air as the lithe brown body goes streaking over a section of close-bitten pastureland; and, urged on by the sound of the hunting horn and the note of the pack, the fox redoubles his efforts. What matters it to him that he is giving amusement to forty-odd people? He is running for his life with pounding heart and starting eyes, harried and almost spent. It will not ease his agony if he is caught and torn to pieces to know that he has been sacrificed in the cause of sport.

But except for the lust of the chase and the thrill of the kill, no thought of the fox enters the minds of those who pursue him. Why should it? Are they not the lords of creation, and therefore entitled to inflict whatever pain and suffering they please on creatures weaker than themselves? Even the vicar hunts regularly, and is as excited as anyone at the kill, so it must be all right!

The fox is tiring. If the hounds can run him down before he reaches Rackman's Wood, there is no chance of his saving his brush. And there is a steep rise to the wood. With the possibility of the kill in sight, Sir Eustace spurs on his horse. The field has whittled down to a handful, for few of those who started have managed to live with the hounds. The long point over grass and plough, divided by quicks and rails and blackthorn, has left them far behind.

The fox realises that only speed can save him, and gathering his failing strength, he puts on a last desperate burst. The wood is close now, and just within the friendly shelter of the trees there is an earth — if that, too, has not been stopped. Almost at the last gasp, with his pelt patched darkly with sweat, he reaches the fringe of the trees. There is something sprawling among the tangled undergrowth — a strange thing that he would like to inspect closer, but he is too hard pressed to pause. The earth is only a yard away, and in a second he is down, his heart well-nigh to bursting, but for the present — safe.

The hounds in full pursuit come streaming into the wood only to stop, whimpering, as they, too, scent the thing that lies so still among the soaking leaves . . .

Sir Eustace Chalebury saw them sniffing amid the undergrowth as he reined in his horse, and came to a not unnatural conclusion.

'Gone to ground!' he cried, swinging round in his saddle. 'Pity. We'll have to dig him out — ' And then, breaking off suddenly: 'My God, it's a man! Here, come and call these brutes off! There's a man here, dead or hurt — '

'A man?' Captain Linden pulled up beside him and stared at the uneasy hounds.

'Yes.' Chalebury nodded curtly, and, dismounting, strode over to the sprawling figure. His face went yellow as he peered down.

'My God!' he exclaimed huskily. 'It's that inspector feller — what's-his-name — Gowper!'

It *had* been Inspector Gowper, but it was nothing now. The dreadful head was crushed and battered, and the blood had turned the rotting leaves on which it rested back to the ruddy tint of autumn.

'This is murder!' whispered Captain Linden, white-faced and horrified. 'Murder! Just like that chap Hicklin' was killed!'

'Go and keep the women away!' muttered Sir Eustace as the rest of the hunt appeared in sight. 'And get someone to go for the police!' He stopped and, reeling back, clutched at his companion's arm, his face so deathly pale that Linden thought he was going to faint.

'Pull yourself together, Chalebury,' he began; and then, he, too, heard it:

'Do ye ken John Peel with his coat so
  gay,
He lived at Troutbeck once on a day,
But now he's gone, far, far away . . . '

It came from the depths of the wood, scarcely audible — and, even as they listened, dying away. The song of the Huntsman!

7

The Ruby Ring

Major Hankin, his thin face anxious and troubled, stood beside Mr. Budd, biting at his lower lip, while Dr. Prowse made an examination of the body. Sir Eustace Chalebury, as soon as he had recovered from the shock induced by the sound of the Huntsman's song, had sent post-haste to the chief constable's house to notify him of the discovery, and that horrified man had immediately called up the Fox and Hounds. Mr. Budd, no less horrified at the news, had met him outside the inn with Leek and the interested Tommy Weston, and stopping only to pick up Dr. Prowse on the way, had hurried as fast as they could to Rackman's Wood.

They had been able to cover part of the distance in Hankin's car, for there was a road from the village that ran within a short distance of the wood; but the rest of the way was only possible on foot. In spite of this, however, they had reached the spot in under an hour and a half from the time the discovery had been made.

'He's been dead for several hours,' said Dr. Prowse, rising at length to his feet and carefully brushing the knees of his trousers. 'The blood is dry. Without binding myself to an hour either way, I should say that he met his death at two o'clock this morning.'

Major Hankin frowned and fingered his moustache. 'Two o'clock,' he muttered. 'What on earth could he have been doing here at such an hour?'

'He said nothin' to you?' Mr. Budd asked.

'Nothing ... That's what I can't understand.'

'Maybe he said something at the station. It's pretty clear that he was on to somethin'. He wouldn't have bin wanderin' about this wood in the middle of a cold night for fun, would he?' He went over and peered down at the thing that had been Inspector Gowper. 'I 'spose these injuries are sim'lar to those in the case of Hicklin'?'

Dr. Prowse nodded. 'Almost exactly. The two crimes appear to me to have been committed with the same weapon — something smooth and heavy,' he mused. 'A loaded stick, perhaps, or something similar.'

'Hm!' the superintendent grunted non-committedly, and he knelt down with difficulty beside the dead man. Slowly and methodically he began to search the pockets. The thick overcoat yielded a battered pipe and a worn pouch, a box of matches, a handkerchief, and an electric hand-lamp. Mr. Budd laid these on one side and continued his search. He took a bunch of keys and a handful of loose change from the trouser pockets, a watch and chain and a fountain-pen from the waistcoat, a wallet from the inside breast pocket of the jacket, and a small, triangular scrap of torn paper. This he examined carefully.

'What have you found?' demanded Major Hankin impatiently.

'Somethin' rather interestin',' murmured the detective slowly. He came ponderously to his feet, still holding the piece of paper. 'The killer took away most of it, but he left this bit behind.'

'What is it?' asked the chief constable quickly.

'It's part of a letter, sir. An' it's the reason that brought poor Gowper to 'is death.' He held it out and Hankin took it. Tommy Weston moved forward and tried to peer over his shoulder, but Mr. Budd interposed his large bulk.

'There's no harm in my seeing it, is there?' said Tommy indignantly. 'I won't publish anything without permission. You ought to know me well enough by now to know that — '

'Well, if you promise not to print anythin' without permission, you can have a peek.'

The reporter hastily availed himself of this generous offer. The scrap of paper consisted of a corner torn from a large sheet, and bore several words hurriedly scrawled in pencil. '*1.45 Rackman's Wood . . . information come . . . alone . . . tell anyone . . .* ' The word 'anyone' was underlined.

'It's pretty obvious that Gowper had a letter or a note from somebody offerin' to supply some information either about the robberies or the murder if he kept an appointment here at 1.45 this mornin',' commented Mr. Budd. 'An' it's equally obvious that the conditions were that 'e was to come alone an' say nothin' to nobody. That's why he kept it to himself, poor feller.'

'And this person, whoever it was, killed him,' muttered the chief constable, staring at the crumpled paper in his hand. 'But why did he kill him?'

'Maybe that's what he wanted him here for, sir,' said the big man. 'He wrote this just to get Gowper to the wood.'

'But why should he have wanted to kill him?' demanded Major Hankin perplexedly. 'What did Gowper know that made it necessary he should die?'

'Whatever it was, I should say Gowper was unaware of it,' Mr. Budd said. 'I mean that Gowper hit on somethin' that was important without knowin' that it was important, if you understand me,' he said. 'He knew somethin' that was dangerous to the safety of the person who wrote that note, but he hadn't yet realised it. But this person knew he knew whatever it was an' wasn't takin' any chances.'

'I see what you mean,' said Hankin thoughtfully.

'I s'pose,' went on Mr. Budd, 'that you don't recognise the writing, sir?'

The chief constable shook his head. 'No,' he answered, and the big man seemed to have expected no other reply.

'Was the inspector a married man, sir?' he asked, and again Major Hankin shook his head. 'Well,' continued Mr. Budd, with a sigh, 'that makes it easier in a way. There won't be nobody to break the news to.'

Tommy Weston shot him a quick glance. He had a sudden conviction that this was not the reason that had prompted the question, though what was in the back of the superintendent's mind he had no idea.

'There was some talk about hearin' somebody singin' in the wood,' murmured Mr. Budd after a short silence. 'They was singin' the theme song of the local spook, wasn't they?'

Major Hankin smiled faintly at this description of the Huntsman, and glanced across to where Sir Eustace was talking to the rest of the hunt, a subdued and rather scared lot of people suddenly sobered by this unexpected contact with violent death. 'Yes, Sir Eustace heard it, and so did Captain Linden and the whips!' he said.

'Queer how this ghost seems ter crop up whenever there is any trouble,' remarked the big man, suppressing a yawn. 'Like a kind of musical background, as you might say — '

'Nonsense!' broke in Dr. Prowse testily. 'The Huntsman can have nothing to do with these murders. It'd take something stronger than a ghost to have inflicted the wounds that killed Hickling and this poor fellow.'

'I see,' Mr. Budd mused. 'Then you're one of the people who think that there's no doubt that the Huntsman is a ghost?'

'I'm one of the people, sir,' retorted the doctor, 'who believes that there are some things unexplainable by ordinary laws, though not necessarily beyond the laws of nature.' He turned away angrily.

Mr. Budd sighed wearily. 'I seem to have upset the old gentleman,' he remarked. 'P'r'aps the Huntsman's a pet of his. Who's this?' He broke off suddenly and stared down the broad ride into the shadows of the wood. Following the direction of his eyes, the others saw the figure of a man coming towards them. It was Henry Cadell!

'Good morning.' He came up to the little group and nodded to Mr. Budd and the chief constable. And then he saw the prone figure amid the stained leaves, and his breath hissed sharply.

'Hello, what's the matter here?' he said quickly. 'Somebody hurt?'

'Somebody dead!' It was Mr. Budd who answered him. 'Inspector Gowper has been murdered!'

'Murdered?' The deep voice held just the right note of horrified surprise. 'When did it happen? How?'

'It happened round about two o'clock this mornin'.' Again it was Mr. Budd who spoke. 'An' as to how, he was killed in the same way that 'Ickling was.'

Cadell lowered his eyes to the body and gave it a swift, comprehensive glance.

'Dreadful!' he said unemotionally. 'This district seems to harbour a particularly savage killer, er, Superintendent. I think that's your rank?'

'It is, sir,' answered Mr. Budd; and then: 'How long have you bin in the wood?'

'Quite a while,' Cadell said. 'Two and a half to three hours, I should think. I'm rather fond of woods. Why?'

'I wondered whether you heard anyone singin'.'

'Certainly I did,' replied Cadell promptly. '*I* was singing!'

'Were you singing 'John Peel'?' demanded the chief constable sharply.

The novelist nodded. 'I was. Why?' A smile twitched his lips. 'Oh, I understand! Somebody heard and thought it was the local ghost, eh?'

'Sir Eustace Chalebury heard you,' said Major Hankin — and Cadell seemed to become aware for the first time of the proximity of the hunt.

'Did they find this poor fellow?' he asked, and when the chief constable nodded: 'It seems to have given them a bit of a shock.

It was a different 'kill' from the one they expected, eh? They wouldn't have minded seeing a fox torn to pieces, but to come suddenly upon a dead man was another matter.'

There was a sneer in his voice, and Hankin was a little shocked. 'Well, naturally,' he said; but the novelist shook his head.

'I don't admit the 'naturally' at all,' he retorted. 'I hold rather strong views on the subject of blood sports, and I consider foxhunting to be cowardly, cruel, and only fit for half-civilised morons. If it's necessary to kill a fox, it should be done humanely, not for the pleasure of a lot of people who can't find anything better to do with their time.'

'I'm afraid,' said the chief constable coldly, 'that you won't find your views very popular in this neighbourhood.'

Cadell shrugged his massive shoulders. 'That'll keep me awake at nights!' he answered. 'To be unpopular with the type of people who inflict pain on a dumb animal for amusement is a compliment!' He gave a curt nod, and was moving away when Mr. Budd stopped him.

'You met nobody else in the wood durin' your walk, sir?' he asked gently.

'No. I saw nobody at all.'

'I think,' went on the big man, staring at him thoughtfully, 'that we've met somewhere before. Now, where could it 'ave bin?'

'I don't think it could have been anywhere,' said the novelist coolly, returning his gaze steadily. 'I've no recollection of ever having seen you before in my life!'

He walked away, and Major Hankin snorted. 'The man's a crank!'

Mr. Budd was saved the embarrassment of a reply — which was just as well, considering that he entirely agreed with Cadell's views — by the arrival of Sir Eustace Chalebury. 'You don't want me anymore, Hankin, do you?' he said, entirely ignoring the others. 'I'd like to get back. There's no sense in hangin' about here.'

'No, there's no reason why you should stay, Chalebury,' said the chief constable, and Sir Eustace cantered away.

'Well, sir,' said Mr. Budd, 'I s'pose

there's nuthin' much we can do, either. How long will the ambulance be?'

Major Hankin had dispatched a message to the police station before leaving the village, with instructions for the primitive hand ambulance to follow him. 'It ought to be here any moment now,' he replied; and he had barely finished speaking before it appeared, accompanied by a sergeant and a constable.

The body of Gowper was lifted gently and placed on the wheeled stretcher; and Mr. Budd, more from the habit of training than because he expected to find anything of importance, made an examination of the place on which it had been lying. He found nothing, and was straightening up when a glint of something red caught his eye. Stooping again, he saw that the object which gleamed was a ring, half-hidden amongst the rotting leaves. He picked it up and looked at it curiously. It was a woman's ring — a circle of platinum and a big cushion-shaped red stone.

'What have you found?' asked the interested Tommy Weston.

Mr. Budd exhibited his discovery, and the chief constable uttered an exclamation. 'Good heavens, that's Miss Renton's ring!' he exclaimed. 'Where did you find it? Under the body? How in the world did it get there?'

'That's what I should like to know, sir,' murmured Mr. Budd, gazing at the little trinket in his palm. 'Who's Miss Renton? I'd like to have a word with her.'

8

The Neglected House

The chief constable told them Audrey Renton's story. 'It's a very sad affair,' he concluded. 'She was devoted to her father, and she's never got over his death. You must have seen her at the inquest?'

Tommy Weston became suddenly interested. 'Is she a tall, slim woman with hair the colour of ripe corn?' he asked quickly.

Major Hankin nodded. 'She must've dropped that ring where you found it, Superintendent. There's nothing else to it. She wouldn't have anything to do with poor Gowper's murder, naturally.'

'I'll return the ring to her all the same,' said Mr. Budd, slipping it into his waistcoat pocket. 'Maybe she'll be glad to get it back.'

They walked slowly in the wake of the ambulance to where Hankin had left his car. 'Where does Miss Renton live, sir?'

inquired Mr. Budd as they reached it.

'At Oaklands,' answered Major Hankin. 'It's the house on the hill, just the other side of Newnham's Spinney.'

He offered them a lift back to the village, but Mr. Budd declined politely. 'A walk 'ull do me good, sir,' he said, to the astonishment of Leek. 'I don't get enough exercise.'

'Since when have you come to that conclusion?' demanded Tommy when the chief constable had driven away.

'Since this very moment,' answered Mr. Budd calmly. 'I'm willin' ter make greater sacrifices than a little pers'nal discomfort in a case of need, an' if I'd let that feller drive me to this woman's house it's ten chances to one 'e'd have come in with me, an' I didn't want 'im to.'

'D'you want me to?' asked Leek eagerly. 'Because if yer don't, I'd like to go back to the — '

'You'll come with me!' broke in his superior severely. 'You ain't to be trusted with that innercent gal at the Fox an' 'Ounds.'

'What's this?' demanded the reporter

with a grin. 'Has Leek got designs on the beautiful Elsie?'

'No, I 'aven't!' said the lean sergeant, flushing.

Tommy gave a whoop of delight. 'Your face has given you away!' he declared.

'He's gone all goofy!' said Mr. Budd disparagingly. 'He'll be babblin' poetry next.'

'I can't imagine him as a Romeo,' remarked Tommy, eyeing the melancholy sergeant critically. 'He looks more like Hamlet in the graveyard scene to me.'

'You was bad enough when that racin' bug hit you,' grunted Mr. Budd, 'but this is worse. You cut out all this romance from your soul an' concentrate on yer job. You're in the police force, though how you ever got there is a mystery.' He produced one of his thin black cigars from his waistcoat pocket and lit it. 'It's queer what ideas people get about women,' he went on musingly. 'There's that feller, Hankin. Although I found this woman's ring under Gowper's body, 'e's certain she ain't got nuthin' to do with it — jest because she 'appens to be pretty, I s'pose?'

'You're an embittered and soured old man!' said Tommy rudely. 'I agree that woman is — '

'An angel in disguise!' growled the big man. 'Maybe we shall find her polishin' her halo and brushin' her wings! At least,' he added, 'I shall, because you ain't comin'!'

'Of course I'm coming,' said Tommy indignantly. 'If you don't let me come with you, I'll arrive just as you're in the middle of your interview, and probably spoil everything.'

'You'll prob'ly do that, anyway,' said the stout superintendent. 'Well, you can come if you like, but remember you don't print nuthin' until I tell yer you can.'

They walked on in silence. Presently the reporter caught a glimpse of a rambling building half-hidden by trees on the hillside, and drew the big man's attention to it. 'That's the place,' he said.

Mr. Budd looked about him. 'There must be a road or somethin' leadin' to it,' he said, and a little further on they came upon the entrance to a drive. It was choked with weeds, and the thick shrubbery that lined it on either side was unkempt. Gaunt trees formed an avenue, their leafless branches interlacing overhead making the approach a gloomy tunnel.

'Doesn't look very cheerful, does it?' remarked Tommy, eyeing the entrance without enthusiasm. 'No wonder that woman looked pale and ill. It's enough to make anyone look ill living in a place like this. I suppose she's lost heart since the death of her father.'

'Maybe,' said Mr. Budd shortly, and he led the way up the drive. When they came in sight of the house they saw that it, too, showed signs of the general neglect. The paint was dirty and blistered, the flower-beds a riot of tangled vegetation, the lawn a waste of rank grass, knee-high.

Mr. Budd mounted the crumbling stone steps to the front door, found a rusty iron bell-pull, and tugged at it. From somewhere inside they heard a faint jangle, but that was all. After waiting for nearly a minute, the stout superintendent rang again. They heard the sound of shuffling footsteps, and then the door was opened a few inches.

'Who are you? What do you want?' asked a cracked voice peevishly.

'I want to see Miss Renton — ' began Mr. Budd.

'Well, you can't!' snapped the voice curtly; and the door would have been shut in their faces if Mr. Budd had not deftly inserted his foot.

'Will you tell Miss Renton that Superintendent Budd of New Scotland Yard wishes to see her, and that the matter is important,' he said authoritatively.

'Miss Renton's busy!' snapped the harsh voice. 'If it's anything important, you can tell me.'

'What is it, Mrs. Willoughby?' a clear, pleasant voice broke in on the tail of the harsh one. 'Who are these people and what do they want?'

'It's a man who says he's from Scotland Yard, dearie.' The harsh tones were curiously soft. 'I don't know what he wants.'

'Could I see you for a minute, miss?' said Mr. Budd quickly. 'I've found some property of yours which I'd like to return to you, and I'd also like a word with you, if you don't mind.'

'Some property?' The door was pulled wide and Audrey Renton appeared on the threshold, a frown on her pale face. 'Do you mean my ring?'

'Yes, miss.' Mr. Budd nodded. 'At least, I'm given to understand it's yours. A platinum ring set with a big red stone.'

'Yes, that's mine,' Audrey said eagerly. She hesitated, her eyes moving quickly from one to the other. There was more than a hint of fear in her expression, as Mr. Budd was quick to note. 'You'd better come in,' she said suddenly, and stood aside.

'Thank you, miss,' murmured the detective, and he stepped into the wide hall, followed by Leek and Tommy Weston. A thin, gaunt woman with an amazingly wrinkled face glared malignantly at them as they passed her.

'This way, please,' said the woman, and she went over to a door on the left which she opened. As she ushered them into the long, low-ceilinged room beyond, Mr.

Budd sniffed. The air was full of a queer pungent smell — an acrid odour with a trace of tar in it. He had smelled it even while he stood outside on the step, and the whole house was reeking with it.

Audrey saw that he had noticed it, and offered an explanation and an apology. 'We've just been putting creosote down the drains,' she said. 'I'm afraid it smells rather horrid, but it's infinitely better than the drains!' She forced a smile. 'Now where did you find my ring?'

'When did you lose it, miss?' asked Mr. Budd, his sleepy eyes taking stock of his surroundings. The inside of the house was a decided improvement on the outside. This room into which they had been invited was comfortably furnished and clean.

'Yesterday,' she answered at once. 'I lost it while I was out.'

'I s'pose you've no idea where, miss?' he inquired.

'No,' she said. 'I didn't discover I'd lost it until I got back. It fits rather loosely.'

'I see. Where did you go while you were out, miss?'

A shadow of annoyance crossed her face. 'Does it matter?' she said a little sharply. 'You've found the ring, haven't you?'

'Yes, I've found it,' said Mr. Budd. 'At least, I've found a ring.' He took it from his pocket and held it out. 'Is this yours?'

'Yes, that's mine,' she said instantly. 'Where did you find it?'

'I found it under the body of a dead man,' he said slowly. 'A man who'd been murdered!'

She caught her breath and stared at him in fear. Her face had gone pale, and she was gasping.

'Inspector Gowper was murdered last night, or rather, early this morning,' said Mr. Budd, 'an' when the body was moved this ring was found underneath it.'

'Inspector Gowper?' Audrey's hand went up to her throat as she repeated the name huskily. 'And my ring was found under the — the body? Then I must have dropped it when I was walking through Rackman's Wood yesterday.'

Mr. Budd's heavy lids drooped over his eyes. 'Yes, miss,' he murmured. 'I expect that's what happened.'

'Can I — can I have the ring?' She held out her hand, and after a moment's hesitation he gave it to her. 'Thank you!' she said, and slipped it on her finger. The colour had come back to her cheeks, but the fear still lingered in her eyes. 'Is there anything else you wish to see me about?'

'Not at present, miss,' Mr. Budd answered, and there was a barely perceptible stress on the word 'present'.

When they were once more outside the house, he rubbed his chin thoughtfully. 'Interestin' and perculiar,' he murmured softly. 'That woman an' that house. Did you notice that smell?'

'The creosote?' said Tommy.

'That's what she said it was, but it wasn't creosote. And another thing. How did she know that Gowper was found in Rackman's Wood? I never said where he was found. She lost that ring while she was out an' she didn't know where. But direc'ly I said it had been found under the body, she said she must've dropped it in Rackman's Wood. Queer, very queer. I think that woman is goin' to be worth keepin' an eye on.'

9

The Secret

The old servant came into the long room after seeing the unwelcome visitors off the premises, and looked at the woman still standing by the mantelpiece. Audrey Renton pushed her hair back wearily from her forehead. She had not yet had time to recover from the strain of that interview.

'What did they want?' asked Mrs. Willoughby curiously. 'I tried to 'ear, but I could only catch a word now 'n' agin.'

'They came to bring me my ring — I thought you heard what the big man said at the door?'

'I did; but I thought maybe there was something else. 'E was a detective, wasn't 'e?' Audrey nodded. 'Was them others detectives, too?'

'I don't know — no, the younger one is a newspaper reporter, I believe,' answered

Audrey. She took a cigarette from a box on a side table and lit it with a hand that shook.

The old servant, who had nursed her when she was a baby, eyed the trembling hand sympathetically. 'It's upset yer, ain't it, dearie?' she said. 'I wouldn't 'ave let 'em in if you 'adn't come, an' — '

'It would have been stupid to try to keep them out. As it is, they must wonder — '

'So long as they only wonder, it don't matter,' said the old woman as she stopped abruptly. 'That's all they come for, then, was it? Ter bring back yer ring?'

'That's all.'

'Well, that's a relief, any'ow!' declared Mrs. Willoughby. 'You could 'ave knocked me down with a duster when that fat feller said who 'e was. I thought the 'ole thing 'ad come out.'

'I thought so, too. But I don't think they suspected anything.'

'There ain't no reason why they should. Don't you go worryin' yer 'ead now, dearie. If the ring was all they come for, there ain't nuthin' ter worry about.'

'How can I help worrying?' said Audrey. 'Supposing they *did* find out, it would be dreadful!' She drew nervously at her cigarette and threw it into the fire. 'We've got to be extra-careful while all these detectives are in the district. They found my ring under — under that inspector's body.'

The old woman sucked her breath quickly through her toothless gums, and her wrinkled face showed her sudden concern.

'Under the body, did they?' she whispered. 'But that don't give nuthin' away. They know yer lorst it — '

'It turns their attention to me,' broke in Audrey, frowning. 'It brought them here. That's the danger.'

'Well, it's over now, dearie,' said the old woman soothingly. 'They've bin an' they've gorn, an' they're no wiser than when they come.'

'I wish I could be sure of that,' Audrey muttered.

'Of course they ain't. 'Ow could they be? You're nervy, dearie. I'll go an' make yer a nice cup o' tea.'

She shuffled away, leaving Audrey staring with a troubled face at the fire. Nervy? It was only natural that when they had found out who the ring belonged to, they should have brought it back — and that they should require an explanation for its presence under the body of that dead man. Well, she had given one, and the detective had seemed satisfied. That was all there really was to it. Surely they *couldn't* suspect anything?

She took another cigarette and lit it; and as she blew out a thin stream of smoke, her eyes strayed to the big framed photograph that hung above the mantelpiece. The bronzed, smiling face of the grey-haired man returned her gaze encouragingly. The relationship was obvious. The same shaped nose, the same line of chin, the same sensitive mouth. Audrey Renton had taken more after her father than the mother she had never known. Perhaps it was because her mother had died in giving her birth that such a close bond of affection had sprung up between herself and the handsome man in the picture. He had suffered an irretrievable loss, and had turned for consolation to the child who had unwittingly been the cause.

All the love that might have been divided was lavished on the baby girl and was abundantly returned. The tears gathered slowly in her eyes as memory brought back many little incidents of her childhood: walks in the woods and over the undulating country; thrilling stories of adventure told by the light of the flickering fire during the long winter evenings; exciting trips to London; and the hundred and one things that go to make up a happy, carefree life. And now that was all over. Andrew Renton had always been restless, and in the end had fallen a victim to his own love of strange countries and wanderings off the beaten track.

In that obscure corner of Africa, where few white men had ever penetrated, had come the tragedy which, like the swift passage of a sponge over a slate, had wiped away all joy from Audrey's life. Perhaps time would bring contentment and peace; but that was all she could hope for. Impatiently she brushed the tears from her eyes. The past could not be altered, and she had the present and the future to contend with. The presence of these watchful men in Chalebury was a constant danger. At any moment they might surprise her secret and drag it into the light of day, and that was a possibility that made her shudder to even contemplate.

The detective had not looked very formidable, but there was something about him underlying that sleepy expression that frightened her. And yet he couldn't suspect anything. She had taken every possible precaution. She forced herself to examine the situation dispassionately, and had to admit that her doubts and fears were mostly imaginary. When Mrs. Willoughby brought in the tea, she was almost cheerful.

★　★　★

The fourth visitor did not come to the house until long after darkness had fallen. Mr. Joseph Eales was a lover of darkness, and seldom left his home during the daytime unless it were to regale himself with beer at the nearest pub. For the most part he slept so that he could be alert and wakeful from dark until dawn, busily engaged in those nefarious activities that supplied him with his precarious livelihood.

A sly, furtive, unpleasant man was Mr. Eales, possessing something of the snake in his makeup. He had the snake's flat head and beady eyes, and could move with the same silence and swiftness. He came gliding noiselessly up the gloomy drive at Oaklands, and paused to survey the house.

There was a light in one of the lower rooms, which showed dimly between the division of the heavy curtains covering the window, and Mr. Eales nodded to himself. She was at home, then. He had been pretty sure she would be, for she hardly ever went out these days. The difficulty would be to get past the old woman. He knew how jealously she guarded her young mistress from unwelcome visitors, as he knew most things about the inhabitants of Chalebury, and he was certainly an unwelcome visitor.

His thin lips curled back in a smile that was particularly unpleasant as he thought how unwelcome he was going to be. He had come armed with a flimsy excuse for gaining an interview with Audrey alone; but the sight of that lighted window had given him an idea that might possibly render any excuse unnecessary. With no more sound than the shadows which surrounded him, he moved stealthily over to that streak of light, and peered into the room from which it came.

She was sitting in a chair by the fire, reading. The light from a big shaded floor-lamp behind her fell on her hair, turning it to a halo of pale gold; but Mr. Eales had no artistic leanings, and the picture she presented was wasted on him. For a minute or two he watched her; and then, raising his hand, he tapped on the glass. He saw her start and raise her eyes from the book, and tapped again louder. She got up, walked a little way towards the window, and stopped. Her face was in shadow now, and he could not see its expression, but he guessed that she was hesitating because she was scared. He drummed again peremptorily with his knuckles, and with a swift movement she came over to the window and pulled aside the curtains.

'Miss Renton!' he called to her as she peered out.

'Who is it?' she asked sharply.

'It's me, miss — Joe Eales,' he replied. 'Can I see yer for a minute, miss?'

Her hand went up to the catch. For a second she fumbled, and then pushed the casement open an inch or two. 'What do you want?' she demanded. 'Why couldn't you go to the front door?'

'I wanted ter see yer without anyone knowin'. Can I come in, miss?'

'What is it you wish to see me about?' she asked curtly.

'I'd rather not tell yer 'ere, miss. Can't I come in?'

She eyed the thin, cunning face distastefully. In common with the majority of the people of Chalebury, she disliked and distrusted the man. But it must be something urgent that had brought him, and her curiosity overcame her first inclination to have nothing to do with him. 'Very well,' she said coolly. 'Go round to the front door and I'll let you in.'

'There's no need ter go ter that trouble, miss. I can hop in 'ere easy.' He pulled the window wide and scrambled over the sill.

'Now,' she said, 'what is it?'

And at almost his first words the colour was struck from her face, and she went white to the lips. This man who stood before her, with that hateful smirk twisting his mouth, had discovered her secret — that secret which hung like a cloud over her life, dimming the brightest day and even tinging her dreams with nightmare visions.

10

The Lady from London

A thaw set in that evening, and by nine o'clock it was raining in torrents. They hissed and splashed on the streaming road outside the Fox and Hounds, and beat a noisy tattoo on the roof.

'I thought we should get it,' remarked Mr. Bragg, setting down his tankard. 'A reg'lar downpour, ain't it?'

'Too 'eavy ter last,' said little Taplin. 'But it'll keep a good few indoors.'

'Includin' the 'Untsman,' put in Scowby with a grin. ''E'll want an umbrella if 'e comes out ternight!'

'That's a subjec' I wouldn't joke about, not if I was you, Tom Scowby,' said Mr. Bragg, frowning heavily.

'You're not tryin' ter tell me that the 'Untsman was respons'ble fer these 'ere murders, are yer?' demanded Scowby sceptically.

'It ain't no good tryin' ter tell you anythink, an' it never were.'

'You can't get away from the fac', Tom, that there weren't no trouble round 'ere until the 'Untsman was seen,' said Perkins.

'You won't never get me to believe that a ghost 'as ter bash people's 'eads in ter kill 'em,' Scowby said stubbornly. 'Nor go round robbin' people's 'ouses, neither.'

'There's such things as h'omens,' said Mr. Bragg. 'I ain't sayin' that the 'Untsman killed George 'Icklin' nor poor Mr. Gowper, but I do say that 'is appearance is a warnin', an' that I'll stick to in the face of any argument.'

'What do you think, sir?' Scowby appealed to Mr. Budd, who was apparently dozing over a large tankard of beer in a corner of the tap-room.

The big man opened a sleepy pair of eyes. 'There's a lot to be said for both sides,' he remarked with the solemnity of a Solomon pronouncing judgment. 'I don't believe in such things as ghosts meself, but there's them that do, an' they're entitled to their opinion.'

'Jest what I says,' agreed Mr. Bragg, never having come near to even suggesting anything of the sort.

'They say,' continued Mr. Bragg, 'that 'e was killed in the same way as what George 'Icklin' was.'

'Do they, now?' said Mr. Budd with an air of great surprise. 'Well, they're not far wrong.'

'It's my opinion,' said Mr. Ketler, leaning forward on his bar and joining in the discussion for the first time, 'that there's a lunatic at work.'

'But what about these 'ere robberies?' objected Scowby. 'You can't put them down ter the work of a loony.'

'No more you can,' said Mr. Budd amiably. It was quite obvious that these people were trying to pump him, and he was not going to be pumped.

'I wasn't thinkin' of the robberies, Mr. Scowby,' said the landlord, shaking his bald head. 'There's nuthin' to show that they've got anything to do with these murders.'

'You're right there,' remarked Perkins. 'An' there's nuthin' to show neither what they 'as got ter do with.'

It was the small and diffident Mr. Taplin who ventured to put a direct question. ''As the perlice got any clue?' he asked, blinking at Mr. Budd through his glasses.

'The p'lice have always got a clue,' he replied. 'But you'll understand, gentlemen, that these things are best not discussed in public.'

He contrived to look extremely wise and cautious. Mr. Budd would have been only too pleased if there had been anything to conceal, but there was not. An examination of Gowper's little cottage had brought to light nothing helpful, and, except for the torn scrap of paper, there was no clue to the motive for his murder, or who had been responsible. Taking it all round, it was a most unsatisfactory case — or, rather, cases; for it was impossible to tell whether the murders of Hickling and Gowper were linked with the robberies and the Huntsman, or whether these were three separate and distinct issues.

The door leading into the tap-room

was pushed open, and the huge figure of Henry Cadell came in. The rain was running off his hat in streams, and the macintosh that had replaced the fleecy coat was wet and shiny. 'What a night!' he exclaimed disgustedly as he took off his hat and shook the water from it onto the sanded floor. 'It came down in bucketsful when I was three-quarters of the way here. If I'd known it was going to be so bad, I wouldn't have come out.'

'Take off your coat, sir,' said Mr. Ketler hospitably, 'and hang it up on that there peg over back o' the door. It'll be fairly dry before you wants to use it again, an' by then I expect the rain will 'ave pretty nigh stopped. It can't last long as 'eavy as this. Johnny Walker, is it, sir?'

'Please!'

The novelist divested himself of the dripping garment and adopted the landlord's suggestion. As he hung the raincoat up, he saw Mr. Budd and nodded. 'Good evening!' he said. 'Any further news about that poor fellow who was killed? What was his name? Cowper?'

'Gowper!' corrected the big man, and

shook his head. 'No, sir, I'm afraid not.'

'Queer business,' grunted Cadell. 'So was that Hickling affair. In fact, this place seems to be the centre of queer things.'

Mr. Budd had opened his mouth to reply when the door was thrown open again and a little wizened man, his shabby clothes clinging to his thin body, shuffled in quickly.

'Hello, Joe!' said Scowby with a grin. 'You look wet!'

'I *am* wet!' snarled Joe Eales ungraciously, pushing his way over to the bar. 'Gimme a drink quick — double whisky!'

Mr. Ketler hesitated.

'It's awlright, I can pay fer it!' snapped the other, evidently guessing what was in the landlord's mind. 'Take it outer that!' He thrust his hand into the breast pocket of his ragged coat and slammed a crumpled five-pound note down on the counter.

The landlord's eyes opened wide, and Scowby whistled. 'Come into a fortune, Joe?' he asked.

'Never you mind what I've come inter!' growled Mr. Eales angrily. 'It ain't none o' your business, anyway, see!'

Mr. Ketler picked up the note and examined it carefully. 'It's a good 'un, all right!' he announced in a tone of mild surprise.

'O' course it is!' said Joe Eales impatiently. 'Now 'urry up with that drink! I'm wet through!'

The whisky was pushed over to him, and he gulped it down neat. 'That's better!' he said, smacking his lips noisily. 'Gimme another!'

He was supplied with the second drink, which he drank more slowly, watched by the fascinated people in the bar.

'Well, you seem to 'ave 'ad a good day an' no mistake!' remarked Mr. Bragg, picking up his tankard.

'Not too bad,' said Joe Eales, stowing away the change which the landlord counted out to him. 'An' I'm goin' ter 'ave some more good days, too. Lots of 'em!'

His roving eyes caught sight of Mr. Budd, and for a moment his confidence deserted him. The thin, cunning face became wary, and he hastily averted his gaze. It was a familiar experience with the stout superintendent, and it told him as plainly as if the man had said so that Joe Eales had something to fear.

'Well, I must be off!' said the poacher, swallowing the remainder of his second drink. 'Good night!' He shuffled quickly over to the door and disappeared into the wet darkness outside.

'Now, I wonder what 'e's bin up to,' said Scowby. 'I've never seen Joe Eales with so much money before.'

This assertion was heartily endorsed by the rest, and they were still discussing the sudden wealth of Mr. Eales when Tommy Weston came down from upstairs. He greeted everybody with a cheery 'good evening', and demanded a pint of beer, which he carried over to the corner occupied by Mr. Budd.

'The labour of the day is over, so let the pleasure begin,' he said after he had swallowed a mighty draught of the beer. 'I've written reams of delectable fare for the edification of the masses who eagerly buy the *Morning Wire* to see what's happening in the great world. I shall go down to posterity as the man who put Chalebury on the map.'

'If you've said anythin' you shouldn't have said,' Mr. Budd growled, 'posterity 'ull come to you sooner than you expect.'

Tommy looked round the bar, saw Cadell talking to the landlord, and raised his eyebrows. 'Quite a distinguished gathering,' he murmured. 'A great novelist, a great detective, and the greatest reporter that ever lived!'

'You've missed the star turn of the evenin',' said Mr. Budd, and he told him of the surprising Mr. Eales. 'I'd like to know where he got that money from,' he concluded, 'an' I'm going to 'ave a shot at findin' out. I'll get the number of the note from Ketler, an' it shouldn't be difficult to trace it.'

'It may have passed through several hands before reaching Eales,' said the reporter.

'It looked a fairly new one ter me,' replied the big man, 'although it was a bit crumpled. Anyway, there's no harm in tryin', and it might lead ter somethin'. In a case like this, the only thing you can do is ter chase up these oddities and see what 'appens. That's the difference between real police work an' what you read about in these stories. In them there's clues chucked about all over the place, an' all the detective 'as ter do is to follow 'em up. They must be clues or they wouldn't 'ave bin mentioned. But in real life yer don't know which is a clue an' which ain't. Real detective work's mostly a matter of patience and perspiration.' He drained his tankard and sat down. 'What's that sergeant of mine doin'?' he asked.

'He's gone to bed, I think,' answered Tommy.

'The amount of sleep that feller requires is astonishin',' Mr. Budd declared. 'Not that it makes much difference whether 'e's asleep or awake.' He yawned and looked at the clock. 'What about another?' he suggested.

The reporter picked up the tankards and was moving towards the bar when the sound of a car drawing up outside made him pause. A door slammed, and then a woman came into the tap-room. She was wearing a heavy fur coat and a small hat, and the face beneath was young and pretty. For a moment she stood hesitating on the threshold, and then, rather timidly, she made her way to the bar.

'Have you any accommodation?' she inquired in a low, pleasant voice. 'I've driven all the way from London, and I want to put up for the night.'

Mr. Ketler pursed his lips. 'I've only got a little room at the top of the house, miss,' he said dubiously.

'Anything will do,' she said quickly. 'I'm so tired I don't mind what it is.'

'We're going to have company,' muttered Tommy Weston, turning to Mr. Budd; but that sleepy-eyed man wasn't listening. His attention was concentrated on Henry Cadell, for the novelist was staring at the woman in the fur coat as though he had seen a ghost!

11

The Night Visitor

White Cottage was not really a cottage at all, being a gabled house of ten rooms standing in four acres of garden and woodland. Nearly a century and a half before, however, a cottage had occupied the present site, and when the new house had been built it had retained the old name. It was a picturesque building with a tiled roof, and heavily timbered.

Before Henry Cadell had bought it, it had been empty for some time. The original owners had died, leaving the property to a son who was sheep-farming in Australia. When he, too, had died, the property had come into the possession of Charles Quilter, a distant cousin, who lived in Chalebury. The old man had let it for three years, and finally sold it to Cadell for a price that the novelist privately considered was a bargain. He had moved in at once, bringing with him a man and his wife, who acted as valet-butler and housekeeper respectively, a daily woman from the village completing the small staff.

The rain had dwindled to a fine drizzle as Cadell came up the short drive. His big face was lined and there was a furrow between his bushy brows, for the evening had produced a real shock. Luckily, the woman had not seen him. On recognising her, he had managed to withdraw to a shadowy corner of the tap-room, and, while Mr. Ketler had taken her upstairs to show her a room, he had slipped away. Her sudden appearance in Chalebury was the last thing he had expected.

He let himself in, and was met in the hall by the grave-faced Flecker, a thin, grizzled man, soft-footed and silent. He took the damp raincoat and hat while Cadell stripped his gloves and tossed them on to the table. 'Will you be requiring anything, sir?' he asked.

'No, thank you, Flecker.'

'Good night, sir.'

Cadell murmured a reply and passed

into the large room on the right of the hall in which he worked. It was comfortably furnished with many easy chairs and bookshelves. Near the window stood a large flat-topped desk littered with books and papers, and in one corner was a group of filing cabinets.

Cadell stirred the dying fire into a cheerful blaze, poured out a whisky-and-soda, and, taking a cigar from a box on the desk, carried both over to a chair and sat down. For a long time he sat staring at the fire, smoking thoughtfully, and the clock on the mantelpiece pointed to twelve when at last he roused himself with a sigh, got up, and, switching off the lights, went up to bed.

Stocking-foot, waiting in the shadow of some bushes on the edge of the lawn, saw the last light go out, and moved cautiously nearer to the house. The rain had ceased, but the sky was overcast, and no ray of light from moon or star relieved the blackness. He crept round to the back of the house and paused beneath a small window. From the pocket of his long coat he took a pair of thick woollen stockings and drew them on over his rubber-soled shoes, and then delicately he began to work on the window. The circle of glass came out noiselessly, adhering to the glue-smeared paper. A gloved hand was thrust into the small opening, and the catch was pushed up. The window swung outward, and, without a sound, Stocking-foot hoisted himself on to the sill and disappeared into the silent house.

Henry Cadell stirred restlessly in his bed, muttering in his troubled sleep, and opened his eyes. The room was in darkness, and there was no sound, but something had disturbed him. He grunted impatiently and tried to settle down again, but he realised wearily that he was in for a bout of wakefulness. It was not unusual, for he had been sleeping badly of late. Probably the activity of mind induced by the unexpected appearance of that woman at the Fox and Hounds was accountable. It had taken him long enough to get to sleep, too. And now he was wide awake again. He switched on the light above his head and glanced at the clock on the little bedside table. A quarter to two. He lay back on the pillows and stared up at the ceiling, his mind returning to the presence of the woman in Chalebury. Why?

A faint sound from below reached him. It was not repeated, but it had been unmistakable — the squeak of a door hinge. The door of his study squeaked — he had meant to speak to Flecker about it and had forgotten — and someone had opened it. The burglar, the man they called Stocking-foot, who had been so active in the district!

He was out of bed in an instant and pulling on a dressing-gown. Swiftly he went over to a tallboy, opened a drawer, and took out a small automatic pistol. It was loaded, and he pulled back the jacket, jerking a cartridge into the breech. Face set, he crossed to the door and noiselessly turned the handle. He could hear nothing when he stepped out into the dark corridor, and moved to the head of the staircase. It was not until he was standing in the hall that he received any further confirmation of unauthorised entry, when he heard the sharp splintering of wood. The noise came from the open door of the study, and he crept silently towards it on bare feet.

The room was illuminated by a dim glimmer of light, and a shadowy figure was bending over the big writing-table.

'Keep still, my friend!' snapped Cadell. 'I've got a gun, and I shall use it if you move.'

The man stiffened and turned his head towards the door.

'Unfortunately for you I suffer from insomnia, and the hinges of this door want oiling,' remarked the novelist, advancing further into the room. 'Take that thing away from your face and let me see what you look like.'

Stocking-foot seemed to have been suddenly turned to stone. Only the eyes that showed above the handkerchief covering his face were alive and watchful.

'Do as I tell you!' Cadell put up his hand to the light switch. But before his finger pressed down, Stocking-foot came suddenly to life. With a quick movement he ducked and sprang backward at the same instant. The French windows behind him flew open with a crash and a tinkle of breaking glass as the full weight of his body was flung against them. And then he was gone!

Cadell swore and squeezed the trigger of his automatic, but the three shots he fired must have gone wide, for when he reached the shattered window there was no sign of the intruder.

It was useless attempting to pursue him on his bare feet, and he turned back into the study. The glimmer of light came from a torch lying on the writing-table, and he was examining this when the sleepy-eyed and scared-looking Flecker put in an appearance.

'What's happened, sir? I thought I heard shots.'

'You did — and I fired 'em! We've had a burglar!' explained Cadell. 'And unless I'm very much mistaken, *the* burglar!'

'You — you don't mean Stocking-foot, sir?' Flecker blinked.

'Yes, and I nearly caught him, too.' Cadell set down the torch and bent over the writing-table. 'He didn't have time to do much damage,' he muttered, fingering the splintered drawer. 'You'd better get on to the police.'

'Yes, sir.' Flecker picked up the telephone and asked to be put through to the station, while Cadell stared at the damaged desk with knitted brows. 'They're sending up as soon as they can get hold of the inspector,' Flecker reported presently.

'Good!' said Cadell absently.

'I suppose it was Stocking-foot?' said Flecker, drawing the coat he was wearing closer round him, for the broken window was letting in an icy draught.

'It must have been, unless they breed burglars round here. Go and make some coffee while I dress.'

He hurried upstairs and hastily slipped into some clothes. By the time he returned to the study, Mrs. Flecker, a round, fat woman sketchily attired in a faded flannel dressing-gown, had arisen, and was staring open-mouthed at the broken window. 'Law, sir,' she said fearfully, 'it's a mercy you 'eard 'im. Why, we might all 'ave been murdered!'

'I don't think we were in any danger,' Cadell declared. 'This man isn't a killer — he's just after what he can get.'

He went over to a cupboard and took out a powerful electric lamp. Passing out through the window, he shone the light on the sodden gravel of the path that ran round the edge of the lawn. There were plenty of marks, but they were all smudged and shapeless. Near the grass, however, he found a splash of red, and a little further on another. So one of his shots had hit its target. The man had been wounded!

He followed the trail of blood spots across the lawn to a belt of shrubbery. The bushes had been trampled down and broken, and in the soft mould in which they grew were unmistakable traces of the route taken by the escaping man. But again the prints were slurred and formless. Beyond the shrubbery was a barbed-wire fence dividing the grounds of White Cottage from a small wood, and here Cadell discovered a shred of grey wool adhering to one of the barbs. There was no doubt the night intruder had been the elusive Stocking-foot. Here was proof, unless someone had copied his habits and worn stockings over their shoes.

It was useless following the trail any further, and Cadell retraced his steps to the house. The coffee he had ordered was ready, and he drank the steaming fluid gratefully. He knew what had brought Stocking-foot to White Cottage that night. The only thing that puzzled him was how the man had known it was there . . .

12

The Clue in the Torch

It was nearly three quarters of an hour before the police arrived, the delay explainable by the presence of a yawning Mr. Budd and an equally sleepy, shivering, and resentful Leek. Inspector Dadds, who had taken Gowper's place, had retaliated for his own broken rest by waking the stout superintendent, and he, in his turn, had dragged Leek from a blissful sleep.

Cadell explained the circumstances briefly, and Mr. Budd made an inspection of the house. He found the window by which Stocking-foot had gained admission, and a glance at the method adopted left him in no doubt as to the identity of the burglar.

'Same old glue and newspaper,' he grunted, peering at the neat circle of glass that had been removed. 'I wonder how he carries the glue? In a bottle, I s'pose.' He rubbed his chin. 'Queer, the way these fellers stick to habit. We've caught more of 'em by knowin' their habits than by any other means.'

'Knowing Stocking-foot's habits hasn't helped you much up to now,' remarked Cadell truthfully.

'It will, sir,' replied Mr. Budd. 'I wonder what he expected to find.'

'I don't suppose he expected anything in particular,' answered the novelist. 'He was just out to pick up anything he could find.' He made no mention of the object he had removed from the drawer of the writing-table and carried upstairs to his bedroom, and which he was convinced had been the real reason for the burglar's visit.

'A feller of Stockin'-foot's class don't take chances,' Mr. Budd said. 'He generally knows what he's after. Had you got any particular valuables, money or jewellery that he might have got to hear about, sir?'

'No,' replied Cadell shortly.

'Funny,' mused the big man, 'I can't

understand his taking a risk on the off-chance. He went straight to that drawer, too. Funny!'

'I'm glad it amuses you!' said the novelist sourly.

'It doesn't amuse me, sir — it worries me. It's queer, an' I don't like queer things when I'm dealin' with an ordinary burglar. You say you wounded him?'

'Yes.' Cadell nodded. 'There's a trail of blood spots over the lawn.' He took the stout man to the place and showed him. Mr. Budd inspected the marks with interest, following them to the shrubbery and the beginning of the little wood beyond. The shred of woollen stocking he detached carefully from the barbed wire and put it away in his wallet.

'If this feller's somebody we know,' he remarked to Inspector Dadds, who had accompanied him, 'the fact that he's wounded may be a bit of luck. It'll mark him.'

'Depends where 'e's wounded,' said Leek dubiously. 'If it was in 'is arm, f'rinstance, an' wasn't serious, no one 'ud be able ter tell.'

'That's true,' agreed Dadds.

'All the same, it may prove a valuable clue,' Mr. Budd insisted. 'He's lost quite a lot of blood, so it can't be such a small wound after all. Let's get back to the house.'

When they reached the study, the big man went over to the desk and looked down thoughtfully at the torch Stocking-foot had left behind. 'I s'pose you've handled this, sir?' he murmured.

'I picked it up — yes,' admitted the novelist. 'I didn't think it mattered. He was wearing gloves, anyway.'

'Yes, he would be,' said Mr. Budd disgustedly. 'An' thick woollen stockin's on his feet. No fingerprints, an' no footprints to give 'im away.' He examined the small torch, pressed the button, and peered at the glowing bulb. 'Cheap make,' he commented disparagingly. 'You can buy 'em anywhere.' A sudden thought struck him, and unscrewing the bottom of the little cylinder, he gave it a shake. A small wad of paper fell into his palm, and he uttered a grunt of satisfaction.

'What is it?' asked Inspector Dadds,

coming to his side.

'Maybe it's nothin'. It just struck me that there might be somethin' of the sort. Sometimes when the batteries in these things don't quite fit, people wedge 'em up with anythin' handy. That's what's happened in this case!'

He had spread the folded scrap of paper out flat on the table-top while he had been speaking. It was very dirty and crumpled, and appeared to be a portion of a bill. Printed in blue lettering was the latter part of what looked like the name of a firm, 'WERIES LTD.', and in faded pencil beneath, 'I Fir — '

The superintendent frowned down at this meagre information. At first glance it did not look very hopeful as a clue to the identity to the owner of the torch. He put it away in his wallet beside the twist of woollen stuff. There was no knowing when it would prove useful. 'Well, that seems to be about all we can do for the moment,' he remarked, yawning prodigiously. 'And I'll admit that it isn't much. Still, this is the first time Stockin'-foot's bin seen, and the first time he's left anythin' that even looked like a clue behind him.'

He left Inspector Dadds to make a search of the grounds as soon as it was light, in case Stocking-foot had dropped anything in his hurried flight, and went back with Leek to the inn. Inquiries would be set on foot among the doctors in the district concerning any patient suffering from what might have been a bullet wound, and that might bring in some information. But it was very doubtful if Stocking-foot would make the mistake of consulting a doctor. He was much more likely to attend to the wound himself.

It was nearly dawn when Mr. Budd wearily mounted the stairs to his room and flung himself, dressed, on the bed. Staring at the ceiling, he allowed his mind to wander over the various events that had occurred in Chalebury. It was a method he had adopted before, and more than once these desultory musings had resulted in a fresh angle on the situation.

There had been the series of robberies perpetrated by Stocking-foot, followed by the appearance of the Huntsman. The murder of George Hickling, and the murder of Inspector Gowper. The robbery at Chalebury Court, and the attempted robbery at Cadell's. Interweaving with these was the discovery of the ruby ring under the dead body of Gowper; the queer behaviour of Audrey Renton, and the strange fact that she lived in a large dilapidated house with only one servant; the sudden wealth of Joe Eales; the arrival of the woman who was now, presumably, sleeping under the same roof as himself; the effect her appearance had had on Cadell; and the conviction that the superintendent had met the novelist before.

Was there any connection between the Huntsman and Stocking-foot and the two murders? It seemed very strange that all these things should happen in one tiny village and be disconnected. That woman up at that big house — what was she afraid of? And that smell she had said was creosote — had she said that deliberately to mislead him, or was it a natural mistake? There was a certain resemblance . . .

With a grunt the superintendent sat up, searched for one of his thin black cigars, lit it, and, lying back again, smoked thoughtfully until there were sounds of life in the house below.

13

Startling News

Mr. Budd came down to breakfast to find a reproachful Tommy Weston in the bar-parlour.

'Some friend you are!' said the reporter disgustedly. 'Stocking-foot gets busy during the night, you're notified, and you don't even give me the tip.'

'It's not part of my job to go round wakin' up sleepin' reporters!' said the big man. 'How did you know anything about this business, anyhow?'

'Everybody knows about it. Ketler told me.'

'Oh, everybody knows?' murmured Mr. Budd. 'That's very interestin'. Who's the news distributor in this district?'

'I expect one of Cadell's servants told the baker or the milkman — you know how these things get about. Cadell shot at the man and wounded him, didn't he?'

'So you know that as well, eh?' growled the stout superintendent. 'D'you know what I said to Cadell, an' what Leek said to me, an' what the local inspector said to both of us?'

'I'm hoping you'll tell me that part of it!'

'Well, you can go on hoping.'

'Now, come across! If you tell me what you know, I'll tell you what I know — '

'It's no use tryin' that old game on me, Weston. There's never been a reporter born yet who couldn't give the police important information if they got some in return.'

'The average reporter, probably,' retorted Tommy loftily. 'But if I say I know something, I mean it.'

'If you really know somethin', it's your duty to inform the police.'

'I'm offering to do so! If you don't take advantage of my generous offer, you'll have to wait until you read all about it in the *Morning Wire* tomorrow.'

'You promised you wouldn't publish anythin' without my permission,' accused Mr.Budd.

'That was in relation to anything *you* discovered. I found this out on my own, while you were snoring — '

'I don't snore!' said Mr. Budd. 'Now, what is this thing you know?'

'If you'll tell me what happened at Cadell's early this morning, I'll tell you.'

'If you *really* know anythin' that's worth hearin',' said Mr. Budd grudgingly, 'I don't mind swappin' what I know for what you say you know.'

'It's a bargain!' agreed the reporter instantly. 'Well, here's what I know. That woman who came here last night left the inn when everybody was asleep. I saw her go. She went directly after the place was shut up for the night, and — ' He stopped as Mr. Ketler came in with a laden tray. The landlord was obviously labouring under an intense excitement.

'Good morning, sir!' he greeted. 'Have you 'eard the news about Sir Eustace? 'E was cleanin' a gun last night an' shot hisself in the leg!'

Mr. Budd stared at him for a moment in silence, then: 'Oh, did he?' he murmured softly. 'Now, that's very interesting indeed! When did this happen?'

'Well, I don't rightly know, sir,' answered the landlord. 'Tilkin, the man what serves the court with milk, told me.'

'Did he? What exactly did this feller Tilkin say?'

Mr. Ketler became voluble. Evidently Tilkin had said a great deal, most of which he had heard from the second housemaid, with whom he was on a particularly friendly footing. It appeared that Sir Eustace Chalebury had been very bad-tempered all the evening, and immediately after dinner had betaken himself to the library alone, where he had remained until the household had retired.

Some time during the night the butler, Foss, had been awakened by groans and cries for help and had discovered his master trying to drag himself upstairs. Sir Eustace had explained that he had been cleaning a rook rifle and the thing had gone off, shooting him in the left leg. The wound was not a serious one — the bullet had gone through the fleshy part of the leg; but it was bleeding a good deal, and Dr. Prowse had been sent for. He had dressed the wound and bundled the baronet off to bed with instructions that he was to remain there for two or three days.

'Hm!' commented the superintendent when the tale had finished. 'Didn't anyone hear the sound of the shot?'

'Not so far as I know, sir,' the landlord replied. 'It's quite likely they didn't. One of them small rifles don't make much noise, sir.'

'No, I s'pose not,' said Mr. Budd thoughtfully. 'You'd think, though, that a sportin' gentleman like Sir Eustace would have made sure it wasn't loaded before he started cleanin' it, wouldn't you?'

'You would, sir,' agreed the landlord, 'but it's amazing how careless people can be with such things.' He finished unloading his tray, a procedure which his eloquence had interrupted, and took his departure.

When he had gone, Mr. Budd looked sleepily across at Tommy Weston. 'Shot in the leg — not a serious wound, but it bled a good deal . . . '

'You're surely not suggesting that Sir

Eustace Chalebury is Stocking-foot, are you?' Tommy said. 'Why should a man of Chalebury's position want to turn burglar? Besides, he was robbed himself — '

'That means nothin',' broke in the big man. 'He might be cunnin' enough to do that just to avert suspicion. Here's a feller usin' Stockin'-foot's methods who breaks into Cadell's house, is discovered by Cadell smashin' open his desk, is shot and wounded. The wound isn't serious enough to prevent him gettin' away, but he must've bled pretty freely to leave those traces. The news we have is that Sir Eustace Chalebury has got such a wound an' is supposed to have come by it by accident while he was cleanin' a gun — a sportsman who is used to handlin' firearms. I say that wants a lot of swallowin'!'

'So does the picture of a man like Sir Eustace creeping about the countryside at night in rubber gloves and a mask, breaking into people's houses,' said Tommy.

'I'm not altogether sure it don't stick in my throat, too. Still, it's funny, all the same. Now tell me some more about this woman goin' out during the night.'

'After we'd gone to bed, I sat up for a bit scribbling out a couple of columns for the *Wire*. I'd just finished when I heard a step passing my door. My room, as you know, is close to the stairs that lead to the upper part of the house, and I wondered who was creeping about so stealthily at such a late hour. I opened my door and had a look, and I was just in time to see this woman start to go downstairs. She had a torch in her hand, and in the reflected light I could see that she was fully dressed. I was most curious to know what she was doing, particularly after the expression I'd seen on Cadell's face when she arrived, and the way he scuttled off.'

'Oh, you noticed that, did you?' murmured Mr. Budd.

'I did. The man was clearly shocked. However, back to the woman . . . I waited until she'd reached the bottom of the stairs, and then I followed her. She unfastened the door without making a sound and went out. A mighty strange thing for a woman to do who had driven all the way from London and admitted that she was tired, so I went after her.

'She was hurrying down the road at a hell of a lick, and it was quite obvious she had a definite purpose in view. If she'd any friends in the neighbourhood, she wouldn't have come to the inn; and anyway, this wasn't exactly a reasonable hour to pay a respectful visit. So I determined to find out just what her game was — but I was unlucky. The night was very dark, and suddenly I lost her. I think she must've turned off into a side lane without my noticing. Anyhow, she disappeared completely, and I came back to the inn. I intended to wait up to see her come back, but I fell asleep.'

'More oddities,' grunted the superintendent, rubbing his chin. 'Nobody in this place seems to be capable of behavin' normally — ' He broke off as Sergeant Leek came in. 'I thought you was thinking of spendin' the day in bed!'

'It's only just after eight,' protested Leek.

'When there's work to be done,' said Mr. Budd seriously, 'after eight is late.

I've got a little job for you when you've finished your breakfast.'

'I was 'opin' I could 'ave 'ad the day off,' Leek said. 'I was going to ask you — '

'What do you want the day off for, anyway?'

'I — I just thought I'd like to 'ave a look round the place,' stammered Leek, and he reddened.

'I don't believe you,' said Tommy. 'You've made an assignation with the lovely Elsie!'

'I — I only asked 'er if she'd like to come for a walk this afternoon,' said Leek sheepishly. 'It's 'er 'alf day.'

'An' what did she say?' demanded Mr. Budd.

'She said she'd like to. I think she's taken to me. She's always very nice.'

'I said nobody in this place was normal,' growled the big man. 'Well, the job I'm givin' you won't take long, so there's no reason why you shouldn't go out with her if you want to.'

Leek brightened.

'Now, if you can detach your mind, or

140

whatever you've got in that narrow head of yours, from this woman, p'raps you'll listen to what I've got to say.'

Leek assumed an expression of intense concentration.

'I've found out the number of that note Eales changed last night,' continued the big man, 'an' I want you to go down to the bank as soon as it opens an' see if they can tell you who it was issued to.'

'What note's this you're talkin' about?' asked Leek.

Mr. Budd sighed.

'Of course, you don't know anythin' about it, do you?' he said wearily. 'You don't know anythin' about anythin' — you never did.' He explained patiently. 'Now,' he concluded, 'd'you think you can attend to that without makin' a mess of it?'

'I'll do my best,' said the sergeant, making a note of the numbers in his notebook. 'You want to know who the bank issued this note to?'

'You've grasped it,' said Mr. Budd, and at that moment the buxom Elsie came in with the breakfast. When the meal was over, Leek departed on his errand, accompanied as far as the post office by Tommy Weston, who wanted to telephone through to his paper.

The lean sergeant was lucky, and returned to the Fox and Hounds at half-past ten, very pleased with himself. He found Mr. Budd ensconced in a comfortable chair in the bar parlour, puffing happily at one of his evil-smelling cigars.

'I've found out what you wanted to know,' said the sergeant triumphantly, and he gasped as a wave of acrid smoke caught at his throat. He broke into a violent fit of coughing.

'What's the matter with you, caught the croups?' demanded Mr. Budd. 'What have you found out?'

'The note was issued to — Miss Audrey Renton,' finished Leek with a desperate effort.

Mr. Budd whistled softly. 'Well, now, fancy that.' He frowned at the end of his cigar and yawned. 'And she paid it to Eales,' he went on musingly. 'Now I wonder why?'

14

What Elsie Knew

Sergeant Leek brushed his hair carefully and examined the result in the mirror over his dressing-table. The few stray hairs that refused to remain in place he smoothed down with the application of a pungent-smelling brilliantine which he had acquired that morning from the village chemist's shop. A watery sun was shining fitfully and wanly from a cloudy sky. Leek put on his jacket, adjusted a new tie also acquired that morning from a village shop, and, struggling into his overcoat, descended the stairs to meet Elsie.

She was waiting for him in the entrance, a neat figure in a tweed costume, and he took off his bowler hat gallantly. 'I 'ope I 'aven't kept you waiting,' he said, although he was five minutes early.

'Oh, no, sir.' She smiled. 'Which way would you like to go?'

'I'll leave that to you,' said Leek. 'You know this place better than I do.'

'It's quite a nice walk across the fields to Newnham's Spinney. Would you like to try that?'

He assented, and they set off side by side, watched, although they were blissfully ignorant of this, by a delighted and amused Tommy Weston from the window of the bar parlour. 'Love's young dream,' said the reporter to Mr. Budd. 'The innocent country woman and our designing and sophisticated villain from London.'

The big man grunted and shifted position in his chair before the fire. 'I believe he's serious,' he said.

'Pity he's going to have a rude awakening,' said Tommy. 'The beautiful Elsie is already tokened — as they say — to the young gentleman who delivers our bread.'

'How do you know that?'

'A reporter knows everything. I'm afraid our innocent country wench is a philanderess. It's very sad, but there it is. The country woman is having the town laddie on a bit of string.'

'What did she go out with him for if

144

she's already engaged to this other feller?'

'Why expect me to fathom the female mind?'

The subject of their brief conversation walked sedately on in a rather embarrassed silence. Leek, who was completely unused to female society except for drunks and his rather dour landlady, tried hard to think of something to say, and eventually achieved a most original opening. 'Pretty around here, ain't it?' he remarked.

'It's all right,' agreed Elsie.

'Nicer in the summer, I expect.'

'Much nicer.'

There was another long interval of silence, and it was Elsie who eventually spoke. 'I suppose you've been a p'liceman fer a long time?'

'Well, not so very long,' replied the sergeant. 'About fifteen years, that's all. And I ain't altogether a policeman, you know. I'm a sergeant in the C.I.D.'

'What's that?'

Leek explained the exact status of the Criminal Investigation Department compared with the uniformed branch.

'And your friend — is 'e the same as you?'

'In a manner o' speakin',' said Leek. ''E's a superintendent, but there's very little difference between us really.'

'He's nice, but 'e rather scares me,' Elsie said, after a pause. 'I don't know what it is about 'im, but I could never be friendly with 'im like I am with you.'

Leek's sallow cheeks flushed with pleasure. 'It's a matter of personality, I expect,' he replied. 'Budd's a good feller, an' 'e's clever at 'is job, but 'e ain't got a takin' way with 'im.'

'It must be an excitin' life, findin' out things an' chasin' people. I expect you've had some queer experiences, eh?'

'I've seen a good bit o' life,' confessed the sergeant, 'though it's 'ard work an' dangerous at times, too.'

Elsie nodded thoughtfully.

'I've come within a narrow shave o' losin' me life more'n once,' Leek went on, developing this theme in the hope of impressing her. 'I remember once . . . ' He launched into an account, exalting his own part in the anecdote he was relating, but to his chagrin his companion seemed only mildly interested.

146

'We turn off 'ere,' she said suddenly, breaking in on his rather rambling story and stopping opposite a stile. He helped her over and was continuing where he had left off when she again interrupted him. 'What do you think of these murders an' all the queer 'appening's round 'ere?' she asked abruptly.

Leek was a little hurt. He had been trying very hard to establish himself as a romantic figure. Apart from which, he didn't think anything about the murders, or any of the other things that had taken place in Chalebury. His attention had been so entirely taken up with the woman at his side that he had scarcely given a thought to the business which was the reason for his presence in the village.

He struggled to think of something really intelligent to say in answer to her question, failed, and fell back on an ancient excuse. 'I don't think I'd be within me duty if I discussed it.'

'I don't see that it could do any 'arm tellin' me,' Elsie pouted, 'an' I might be able ter 'elp you.'

Leek was genuinely astonished. 'What

d'you know about it?'

'I didn't say I knew anything,' she answered quickly. 'But supposin' I did — would I get into trouble fer not sayin' anythin' before?'

'It depends,' he said slowly. 'If it's anythin' about these murders that would 'elp the police to find the murderer, you oughtn't ter keep it ter yourself. That's makin' you an accessory after the fac', an' that's a serious thing.'

'But supposin' I wasn't sure that it 'ad got anything ter do with the murders?'

'You still ought ter tell anythin' you know,' answered Leek. 'It's our job to find out whether it's important or not.'

'If I was ter tell you, you'd see that I didn't get in any trouble, wouldn't you?' She looked up at him with an expression that set his heart performing curious acrobatics and rendered him a little breathless. 'An' you could tell the other feller if — if you thought it was worth it, couldn't you? It's bin worrying me ever since I 'eard it, but I didn't like ter say anythin' in case it got the gentleman into trouble.'

148

'What gentleman? You'd better tell me now you've gone so far. I can promise you you won't get into no trouble.'

'Well . . . ' She spoke reluctantly, as though she was rather sorry she had broached the subject, after all. ' . . . it's about Sir Eustace an' George 'Ickling. I suppose I really ought to have spoken out before, but I — I couldn't make up me mind. It was only when you asked me ter go fer a walk with you that I thought it would be a good chance, because it's really bin worryin' me something cruel. I was goin' ter tell the stout gentleman the other mornin', an' then somehow I couldn't.'

'You tell me,' said Leek gently. 'It'll be my respons'bility then — see?'

'It was the — the night that George 'Ickling was killed,' she began hesitantly. 'It was my night off, an' I was goin' ter meet 'Arry — Mr. Norris — my fiancé — '

'Are you engaged, then?'

'Yes. Didn't you know?' she answered; and his heart sank. 'I've bin engaged nearly eighteen months. I thought everybody knew. I was goin' ter meet Mr.

Norris — he lives on the other side of the village, an' I usually call fer 'im — an' I was passin' the end of Oak Apple Lane, when I 'eard Sir Eustace's voice. You couldn't mistake it, 'e was talkin' so loud. 'You'll be sorry for this!' I 'eard 'im say. 'I'll see you in hell before I'll pay a penny, you — ' I can't tell you what 'e said — it was a dreadful word. 'You'll be sorry first!' answered another voice, an' I knew it was George 'Ickling what spoke. 'An' don't be so free with yer — ' He repeated what Sir Eustace had called him. Then they saw me — they was standin' jest inside the entrance to the lane — an' they shut up.

'That's all, but I wondered what they was 'avin' a row over, an' it's worried me ever since. I suppose I ought to 'ave told Mr. Gowper, but I didn't like to. I didn't want ter get a gentleman like Sir Eustace inter trouble — though it did seem funny that he should have spoken like that to one of 'is gardeners, an' that George 'Ickling should 'ave answered 'im like 'e did.'

'You're sure it was Sir Eustace?' asked

Leek dully. The mention of Mr. Norris had destroyed the rosy dreams that had enveloped him, and their place had been taken by a curious apathy.

She nodded. 'Oh yes, it was Sir Eustace all right,' she said with conviction. 'An' it was George 'Ickling, too. Don't you think it was funny, seeing what 'appened to 'im that very night?'

'Yes,' said the lean sergeant tonelessly. 'I wish you'd said somethin' about it before.'

'Well, I've told you now, an' you can do what you like about it.'

They walked on in silence, came to the end of the footpath, and climbed another stile. 'I suppose,' said Leek with a sigh, as he helped his companion over, 'that you'll be seein' this feller Norris this evenin'?'

'Yes,' she answered. 'Why?'

'I shouldn't say anythin' to him or to anyone else.'

'I haven't told anyone except you,' she replied. 'I told you because — well, because I had to tell someone, an' I thought you'd understand how I felt about it.'

'I see.' He wondered if she knew how

he felt about the sudden shattering of his brief romance. She had only accepted his suggestion for a walk because she had made up her mind to confide in him.

By the time he said goodbye to her outside the Fox and Hounds, Leek had recovered something of his normal outlook. Elsie hurried away to keep her appointment with the fortunate Harry Norris, and the sergeant, his short interlude of illusion over, went in to acquaint Mr. Budd with what he had learned.

15

The Mysterious Miss Renton

'It's all very involved an' complicated,' remarked Mr. Budd, pulling irritably at his large nose. The sergeant had found him alone, dozing in front of the fire in the bar-parlour, and had just related his news.

'It looks as though this feller Sir Eustace had a motive fer wantin' ter get rid of 'Icklin', don't it?' said Leek.

'It does,' Mr. Budd agreed. 'It looks as though Hicklin' had been tryin' a little blackmail which didn't come off. An' if I was the kind of feller that jumped to conclusions, I'd go further an' say that Hicklin' had discovered that his employer was Stockin'-foot, an' had threatened 'im with exposure.'

'If you ask me,' said the sergeant, 'it all fits perfect.'

'That's the trouble — it *don't* fit

153

perfect,' said his superior. 'There's pieces that don't fit at all. There's the woman up at that house, an' Joe Eales an' his five-pound notes; there's Cadell, an' this other woman who suddenly turns up from London an' goes creepin' out when she thinks everyone's asleep; an' there's that ring under the body o' poor Gowper. An' there's the Huntsman, gallopin' about the country at night an' singin' his theme song. I've never come across such a whole lot of disconnected bits an' pieces before in me life! Murders an' robberies an' ghosts! I knew that woman knew something though, an' I'm glad you got it out of her.'

'She agreed ter come out with me so that she could tell me,' said Leek miserably. 'Did you know she was engaged?'

'Weston told me this afternoon. Don't let it bother you too much, Leek. A wife's a great blessin' sometimes, an' sometimes she's just the reverse. You're better off as you are.' His tone was so unusually kind that the sergeant stared. 'You was serious about 'er, wasn't you?' went on Mr. Budd. And when Leek nodded: 'An' it's

154

given you a bit of a shock ter find that she's already fixed up with someone else. The same thing 'appened ter me once. You'll get over it — an' the best way of getting over it is work. Pop off an' have a sleep. We shall probably be out half the night.'

'Where are we goin'?'

'Explorin',' Mr. Budd answered slowly. 'I'm very anxious to see that house of Audrey Renton's by night.'

'What for?' Leek demanded, astonished.

'Think of that big house bein' lived in by one young woman and an old woman. No servants, no gardeners, no visitors. It's all wrong; an' when things are all wrong, I like to know why.'

''P'r'aps she don't keep servants because she can't afford it.'

'That ain't the reason. She's quite well off — her father left her a lot of money. She's never got over his death — maybe that's the reason; an', again, maybe it isn't. You can see it was a nice place once, with well-cut lawns an' beds full of flowers. An' she uses creosote to clean out the drains — only it isn't creosote.' He yawned. 'I've bin thinkin' hard all the afternoon, an' I'm convinced that we ought to pay a visit to Oaklands tonight.'

'What do you expect ter find?'

The stout superintendent blew out a stream of pungent smoke. 'I don't know,' he replied thoughtfully. 'Somethin' that's queer, because I've got a hunch that Miss Audrey Renton is up to some very peculiar tricks. It's my opinion that she knows quite a lot about the strange things that have been happening in Chalebury.'

16

Through the Window

Sergeant Leek's thin face twisted into a dubious expression. 'You ain't suggestin' that she's Stocking-foot, are yer?'

'Of course I'm not. Stockin'-foot's a man, an' a professional crook; but there's other things goin' on round here besides Stockin'-foot, an' I'm not at all sure that these other things ain't more important. On the one hand we've got a plain, straight-forward, country-house robber — nothin' particularly extraordinary about 'im — an' on the other, we've got ghosts an' murders, an' people behavin' themselves in a queer way. That *is* extraordinary, an' the most extraordinary of all is this woman. She ain't natural, an' it's my experience that when a person ain't natural there's a reason for it.'

'There may be,' said the sergeant, 'but it may not have anything ter do with the rest of it. Most likely she's got some sort o' family trouble — '

'All the family trouble in the world won't account for the fact that she knew Gowper had been killed in Rackman's Wood without bein' told,' interrupted the big man. 'She's hidin' something an' she's scared. Meantime, don't go sayin' anythin' to anybody. I don't want to advertise the fact that I'm interested in her.'

'Of course I won't say anythin'!' protested Leek indignantly. 'What time are we going on this job?'

'We'll leave here about nine — I think that'll be early enough — an' we'll sneak out without letting Weston know where we're goin'. I don't want him.'

This proved to be easier than he expected, for Tommy Weston had his own plans for that evening, which he was particularly anxious should not be shared with his official companions.

The night was very dark when they left the Fox and Hounds, and although it was not raining, the air was damp and chill. Leek drew his overcoat closer round him. The prospect of prowling about the neglected garden at Oaklands did not appeal to him as an ideal method of spending a winter's evening. Mr. Budd, apparently oblivious to the inclemency of the weather, plodded ponderously along in silence. It was a considerable distance from the inn, and a clock in the village was chiming the three-quarters when they came to the entrance to the drive.

'Here we are,' whispered the superintendent. 'Keep on the grass, an' don't go fallin' over anythin'.' He led the way up the gloomy avenue, with the lean sergeant following closely at his heels. They reached the bend and saw a faint light ahead. The house itself merged so completely with the surrounding darkness that but for that streak of light it might not have been there at all. As they drew closer, the big man began to pick his way carefully among the trailing briars and general debris of the ruined garden, and presently halted by a patch of shrubbery that commanded a view of the lighted window and the porch. It was the same patch of shrubbery, although he did not know this, from which Joe Eales had watched on the evening when fortune had smiled on him.

'You just stop 'ere,' Mr. Budd instructed. 'I'm goin' to have a look inter that room if I can.'

He moved away from the sergeant's side and noiselessly crossed the intervening strip of weed-covered path. At last he reached his objective and peered through the slit in the curtains. What he saw was very much the same as Mr. Eales had seen. Audrey Renton was sitting in an easy chair before the fire facing the window, the light from a shaded lamp behind her falling in a golden circle of which she was the centre. The rest of the large room was in shadow, and at first glance Mr. Budd thought she was alone. And then he saw a movement in the chair opposite her, and caught a glimpse of a black-clad arm. That was all he could see of the other occupant of the room.

The deep rumble of a man's voice came faintly to his ears, and the woman shook her head. Her lips moved, and she began to speak rapidly, augmenting what she was saying with emphatic gestures.

The big man could hear nothing that was intelligible; but from her expression he guessed that the unknown visitor had proffered a suggestion that had been received unfavourably. Again the low mutter of the man's voice reached him, and from the general tone it was evident that he was arguing. The woman shook her head once more and broke in with a torrent of words. She seemed to be trying to make her companion see some point of view that he strongly disagreed with.

The argument continued, and the watchful Mr. Budd wondered what it was all about. Who was the man in the chair, and what was he endeavouring to persuade the woman to do? But she apparently succeeded in convincing him that she was right, for presently she relaxed her rather strained attitude, and the stout superintendent almost heard her sigh of relief as she took a cigarette from a box beside her and lighted it. The conversation between them continued at a more normal level for a little while; and then, as Mr. Budd had been hoping he would eventually, the visitor rose to take his departure. As he came into the light, the detective saw the lined face and the high forehead, with the snow-white hair. It was Dr. Prowse!

He had been prepared for almost anybody but the doctor, although there was nothing extraordinary in his being there. He had probably known Audrey Renton since childhood — had most likely been a friend of her father's — and it was only natural that he should visit her. Quite possibly he had come in a semi-professional capacity. Audrey Renton was living an abnormal, unhealthy life, shut up in this great house with only the old woman for company. As a doctor he would undoubtedly disapprove and use his best endeavours to make her change her habits. Just the kind of thing that a doctor and an old friend would do. She should be out and about, mixing with people of her own age instead of moping about this depressing place, with its atmosphere of neglect and decay. It was enough to make her thoroughly ill, if her appearance was anything to judge by. And there was no real reason for it. One could respect great grief, but not such ridiculous eccentricity. Always supposing, of course, that grief *was* the reason for it.

The woman and the old man had gone out into the hall; and after a short pause, during which Mr. Budd could visualise him putting on his overcoat, the front door opened and a dim fan of light streamed over the steps. The superintendent crouched down under the sill of the window as the vague figure of the doctor loomed into the patch of illumination.

'Goodnight, my dear!' The deep voice came floating clearly to his ears. 'I'll come and see you again tomorrow. In the meanwhile, don't forget what I've said. Exercise and fresh air are essential. You must arrange for that.' He added something which Mr. Budd did not catch, and turned away. The door closed, and the receding footsteps of the doctor faded away down the drive.

Mr. Budd straightened up and again applied his eye to the chink in the curtain. The woman came back into the room, and, crossing over to the fireplace, stood looking down into the flames. Her attitude was tired and weary, and after a moment or two she dropped her head onto the arm that was resting along the mantelpiece, and her shoulders shook.

She's on the verge of a complete breakdown, thought Budd. *I suppose Prowse saw that. But what is it that's upsetting her? It can't be her father's death — it must be something more recent. Now, what's she been up to?* He watched curiously and not unsympathetically as Audrey recovered from her momentary weakness, dried her eyes on a wisp of handkerchief, and passed a small powder-puff over her face. When she had done this she stooped, picked up the poker, and stirred the fire. The ruddy light shone full on her face, and Mr. Budd was startled at the expression of utter despair that he saw there. She was supporting a burden that was well-nigh intolerable, and she was breaking under the strain.

For a minute or so she crouched in front of the fire, and then she went over to a small cabinet on the other side of the room. Mr. Budd could not see what she was doing, but when she came back she held something white in her fingers. He saw that the white object was a pair of gloves. Was she going out? It certainly looked like it, for she began slowly to pull the gloves on. And then he saw that they were not ordinary gloves, but *rubber* gloves!

Was this the preliminary to some kind of cleaning operation? It was a queer time to start — getting on for eleven o'clock. She left the room, returning after a short interval with a large bundle wrapped in a white sheet, which she put down in front of the hearth. Mr. Budd's frown deepened. Was she going to clean some article of wearing apparel? If so, it was surely an odd time, and why clean it herself? An answer flashed to his mind almost before the question had faded. She had chosen this time because there would be nobody about to see her; and she was doing it herself because the stains on that clothing were such that it would be impossible to explain them away — bloodstains!

Before his eyes rose a picture of the body of Gowper lying among the rotting leaves, and the ring he had found under it. He heard Audrey say again, 'I must have dropped it when I was walking through Rackman's Wood yesterday.' Was this the secret that was weighing so heavily upon her?

She had opened the bundle, and he saw that he had been right when he had concluded that it contained clothing. But it was not women's clothing. He caught a glimpse of a shirt and trousers, a jacket and waistcoat. She fetched a pair of scissors and began methodically to cut the garments into strips, which she fed to the leaping flames in the grate — and her face as she did so bore such an expression of loathing and disgust as Mr. Budd had never before seen in his life!

17

'Blackmail's a Dangerous Game!'

For several days after his night visit to Oaklands, nothing happened to further Mr. Budd's investigations. Stocking-foot remained inactive, the Huntsman was neither seen nor heard, and no further clues came to light in respect of the two murders. The inquest on Gowper was held and adjourned, and although there was still a considerable amount of gossip rife, the village settled down to a period of peace. But it was to be rudely shattered before very long with a sensation compared to which the previous events were as water to wine.

Mr. Budd pursued such inquiries as were possible with a dogged persistence that was worthy of better results. The torn portion of the letter that had brought Gowper to Rackman's Wood and his death was compared with the handwriting of most of the people in the village, but there was no resemblance between that pencilled scrawl and any of the specimens that Mr. Budd and the police had succeeded in collecting with so much labour.

A further and more thorough examination of the scrap of paper found in the torch left behind at Cadell's by the burglar yielded no more information than it had done in the first instance, and was destined not to, until accident showed the stout superintendent what a vital clue it contained. An interview with Sir Eustace Chalebury, obtained through the medium of Major Hankin, concerning what Elsie had overheard on the night Hickling had met his death, ended like the rest, in nothing that was the slightest help. The interview took place in the baronet's bedroom, and Sir Eustace admitted, without any hesitation, that he had met the gardener that evening.

'The feller was drunk,' he declared, glaring at Mr. Budd from among his pillows. 'He stopped me in Oak Apple Lane and demanded a rise of wages. I told him I'd see him in hell first, and he got abusive. I said I'd talk to him when he was sober, and left him. That's all there is to that.'

'Why didn't you mention this meetin', sir, before?' asked Mr. Budd gently.

'Because until you reminded me of it, I'd forgotten,' replied Sir Eustace curtly. 'Anyhow, it wasn't important. If Hicklin' hadn't been killed, I should have sacked him, an' that would have been the end of it.'

'Instead of which, sir,' said Mr. Budd dreamily, 'it's only the beginnin' of it. Well, I'm sorry you can't help me at all.'

Mr. Budd and the chief constable took their departure. 'Have you any hope of finding this man?' asked Major Hankin as they were shown out by Foss.

'Yes, I think I shall find him,' said the detective, 'though it may take a bit o' time. It's all the more difficult because there's such a lot of other things as well goin' on. You can't sort out which is which.'

'The village seems to have recently become a hotbed of crime,' Hankin declared gloomily. 'Robbery, murder, and — '

'Blackmail,' Mr. Budd ended softly.

The chief constable stopped in the act of getting into his car and stared at him. 'Blackmail? What do you mean?'

'There's a feller called Joe Eales who's bin spendin' a lot o' money lately — chuckin' five-pound notes around.'

Hankin frowned. 'The little poacher fellow? Where did he get them from?'

'They was issued to Miss Renton,' answered Mr. Budd.

'Are you suggesting that Eales has been blackmailing Audrey Renton?'

'It looks very like it to me,' said the Superintendent. 'These notes was issued by the bank to Miss Renton, an' now Joe Eales is spendin' 'em.'

'But what reason could Eales have for getting money out of Miss Renton by blackmail?'

'I can't tell you that, sir, but there must be somethin'.'

'It's absurd — ridiculous!' muttered Hankin, biting at his lower lip. 'I've known Audrey Renton since she was a child. She can't — ' He stopped, rubbed angrily at his moustache, and then, suddenly making up his mind: 'We'll go and see this fellow Eales, now, and ask him to explain where he got this money from, and why.' He got into his car and motioned Mr. Budd to the seat at his side.

'I think,' began the superintendent, 'that it might be better — '

'I know this feller,' broke in the chief constable. 'A nasty little rat of a man. We've had trouble with him before — petty theft and drunkenness. If there's anything in this idea of yours, we'll make him talk.'

He sent the car speeding down the drive, and Mr. Budd relapsed into silence. It was not the way Mr. Budd would have gone to work on his own; he preferred a more subtle approach. If Eales refused to speak, and Audrey Renton backed him up — in other words, if she offered an explanation for having given him the money, whether it was the true one or not, and stuck to it — they were no better off. In fact they would be worse off, for they would have shown their hand. He put forward this argument during the journey to Joe Eales's cottage, but Hankin refused to see his point. His military training had imbued him with a liking for direct methods.

They reached Mr. Eales's cottage, and the chief constable pulled up. There was no sign of life about the tumbledown place. The door was shut; the broken, dirty windows stared back at them blankly. Mr. Budd squeezed himself out of his seat and stepped gingerly down onto the rutted road, followed by Hankin. There was no gate to Mr. Eales's abode, and the path beyond ran through a waste of nettles and weeds to the dingy, blistered door under a rotting porch.

Major Hankin walked up the path and rapped sharply on the door with his knuckles. There was no reply, and he knocked again. No result. He snorted irritably. 'He's either out or he's drunk — probably the latter.' He stepped back a couple of paces and eyed the dilapidated shack in frowning annoyance. 'Well, we can't very well break in — ' he began, when the slow voice of Mr. Budd interrupted him.

'There's no need to break in, sir,' he said. 'The door's not fastened.' He had pressed down the old-fashioned latch and the door had opened under his hand.

'Then he must be somewhere about,' said Hankin. He peered into the dark, evil-smelling passage and called sharply: 'Eales, are you there?'

No answer, no sound of any sort.

'He's *not* here,' said the chief constable. 'We've had our trouble for nothing, I'm afraid.'

'Not entirely, perhaps,' remarked Mr. Budd. 'Now we're here, we may as well look round the place. There might be somethin' interestin'.'

'I don't know whether we ought to do that,' said Hankin with the ingrained respect which the law has for property. But Mr. Budd was already inside, and after a momentary hesitation, the chief constable followed him.

The big man fumbled for a box of matches and struck a light. The tiny glimmer revealed a partly closed door on the right, and this he pushed wide. The room beyond was small and ill-furnished. The light from the dirty window showed the almost unbelievable squalor of the place. There was a bare table spread with the remains of a meal, a broken chair, and a rickety dresser. The floor was bare and indescribably filthy, and apparently no attempt had been made to clean the place for months.

Mr. Budd uttered a sudden sharp exclamation and was bending forward peering at the floor. Amid the general grime was a spot of red. Near it was another and another — a spattered collection of crimson drops.

'What is it?' asked Hankin. 'Blood?'

'Yes, sir,' Mr. Budd answered. 'There's quite a lot of it, too!' He pointed to another patch near the window.

'So that's why Eales isn't here,' muttered the chief constable. 'He must have met with an accident.'

'Yes, sir, I think he has. What I'm wonderin' is, who was responsible for the 'accident'? Blackmail's a dangerous game, sir. In my opinion this feller Eales has been too clever, but not quite so clever as somebody else has been. I don't like the look of things at all.'

18

'Gone Away!'

Mr. Budd's gently spoken words faded to a silence that seemed to fill the dark little room in Eales's cottage with an unpleasant sense of tragedy. Quite suddenly the atmosphere had become sinister and charged with a vaguely horrible portent. The remains of the meal on the table, the unlocked door, and the splashes of red mingling with the grime on the floor took on a different and a more dreadful significance.

'The fact that Eales isn't here means nothing,' said Hankin, obviously determined to find a simple explanation if he could. 'If he hurt himself badly, he may have gone to see a doctor.'

'These spots of blood are dry,' put in the big man, stooping laboriously and touching one of the stains with a podgy finger. 'They must've bin made very early in the night. If he isn't here because he hurt himself an' went to see a doctor, it seems to me that it's taken him a long time.'

'He may not have gone at once. Perhaps — '

'He didn't finish his supper,' interrupted the stout superintendent gently, turning his sleepy eyes toward the table. 'He didn't finish his supper, an' he left his beer.' He pointed to a half-full glass of beer that had gone stale and flat. Hankin pursed his lips.

'He knew something,' said Mr. Budd. 'He was putting the 'black' over on that woman — there ain't much doubt of that.'

'I can't believe that Miss Renton can have had anything to do with this — this disappearance of Eales, which is what your suggestion amounts to,' said Hankin, frowning and shaking his head. 'There must be some quite simple explanation for the man's absence. Perhaps he's just cleared out of his own accord?'

'In the middle of his supper, an' without waitin' to drink his beer?' said

Mr. Budd sceptically. He began to wander about the room, peering at the meagre household goods of the absent owner, while the worried and still-doubtful chief constable stood scratching a little irritably at his moustache. Suddenly Mr. Budd uttered a grunt, and, stretching up his arm, took something from one of the dirty shelves of the dresser.

'This proves that he ain't gone intentionally, sir,' he said. 'He might leave 'is supper an' beer, but he wouldn't leave *this* behind him! Two five-pound notes an' three pound notes. If Joe Eales don't come back now, we'll know somethin's 'appened to him.'

And Joe Eales did not come back. The day passed and the night came, and there was no sign of him.

★ ★ ★

'It looks as though you were right,' said Major Hankin when Mr. Budd saw him that evening at the police station. 'We've circulated a description of the man and asked for any information concerning him. If that doesn't bring any results, I shall be convinced.'

'I'm convinced now, sir,' answered Mr. Budd. 'Joe Eales has been got out of the way.'

The chief constable passed a hand over his thinning hair, and the lines in his forehead deepened. 'I still can't believe that Audrey Renton can have had any hand in it,' he murmured almost to himself.

'She drew out a hundred pounds from the bank,' said Mr. Budd, 'an' most o' that money's been traced to Eales. What did she give it 'im for?'

'I'll admit it seems obvious that he was blackmailing her,' said Hankin, 'but she would never have gone to the length of — of — '

'Of doin' whatever's been done to Eales,' finished the big man as he hesitated. 'Well, perhaps somebody else is responsible for that — somebody who's mixed up with Miss Renton in this business, whatever it is.'

'But what's she been up to that could've put her in the power of a man like Eales?'

'I don't know, sir. I only know that there's some queer business somewhere, an' that she's in it.'

'Suppose we see her and ask her?'

'I'd much rather not, sir,' said the stout superintendent quickly, breathing an inward prayer that the chief constable would not insist on this proceeding. 'It might do a lot more 'arm than good. If she's bin up to anything serious she's not likely to tell us, an' it would only put 'er on 'er guard.'

'She can't have done anything very serious,' snapped Hankin. 'That's nonsense.'

'Is it?' murmured Mr. Budd. 'There's several very serious things happened in this district lately, includin' two murders. S'posin' Miss Renton's got mixed up with what's behind them — '

'Nonsense, man! Miss Renton's lived here ever since she was a child. How could she have got mixed up, as you call it, with the person or persons who killed Hickling and Gowper?'

'Queerer things have happened,' said Mr. Budd, completely unabashed by the other's vehemence. 'Maybe the killer's a friend of Miss Renton's an' she's shieldin' him. P'raps that's what Eales knew. Anyway, she knows somethin', an' I'd rather she wasn't scared off just at the moment, sir.'

'Very well,' agreed Major Hankin grudgingly. 'I suppose you'd better have your own way.'

After a brief word with Inspector Dadds, who came in at that moment concerning the missing Mr. Eales, the big man left the little station-house and walked slowly towards the Fox and Hounds.

Mr. Budd lit one of his cigars and strolled along, pondering over his problem. His reports to the Yard had up to now been short without being very sweet. Colonel Blair was not going to be satisfied for long without tangible results to justify his continued presence in Chalebury. He would be recalled and there would be a severe reprimand for his failure.

He came to the end of the high street and hesitated. The quickest way to the inn was a short cut through a narrow lane and a footpath that skirted Long Meadow and came out on the old post road. It saved nearly a mile, and Mr. Budd was in favour of anything that saved him unnecessary exertion. His hesitation was due only to the fact that the lane and footpath were very dark. His habitual laziness won. He turned off into the lane.

At length Mr. Budd reached the end of the lane and the beginning of the footpath. When he had laboriously climbed the stile that separated the two, he ran over in his mind the various people he had come in contact with, and paused at the name of Cadell. What was he doing in Chalebury at all? He had bought White Cottage and settled down to live there, but why? He not only disliked hunting, he was almost a fanatic on the subject. Then why, with all the rest of England to choose from, had he come to live in Chalebury, where hunting was the chief interest? A man who disliked the sea would hardly buy a house in Brighton.

Cadell, then, had come to live in Chalebury, not because he liked the district, but for some ulterior motive. He had come to live in Chalebury because, of all places in England, it was the one place that suited his purpose. What was that purpose? It wasn't the business with which his name was associated. A writer can do his work anywhere he pleases. It wasn't because of the people in the neighbourhood. He and they had nothing in common, and he knew none of them. Why, then, should he have come to the district at all? The answer came almost unbidden: because there was something or someone in Chalebury that could be found nowhere else.

Mr. Budd stopped in the middle of the narrow footpath and whistled softly. Was he really on to something important at last? Cadell had arrived in the village on the same day that had seen the end of George Hickling.

Someone or something — which? It was more likely to be someone who was already there; someone who was likely to remain for a long time, since Cadell had bought White Cottage. Audrey Renton — was *she* the magnet that had drawn Henry Cadell all the way from London to settle in this little village in the shires?

The woman who lived alone in that big house, whose ring had been found under the dead body of poor Gowper, who had paid a hundred pounds for no apparent reason to the missing Joe Eales, and who burned men's clothes at night. Was there a connection between these two other than the fact that they both behaved oddly? There was a mystery about Cadell, and there was a mystery about Audrey Renton. Did the mysteries intermingle?

Once again Mr. Budd strove to capture the elusive memory that was flitting about in his brain. Where had he seen the novelist before in circumstances that suggested unpleasantness? It was a very long time ago. He was still striving vainly to recollect the occasion when he reached the Fox and Hounds, and was greeted by Leek with news that added one more mystery to his ever-increasing stock.

19

The Forged Notes

The tap-room held its usual regular habitués when he came in, but there was no sign of Cadell. Since the arrival of the woman on that wet and dreary night, he had kept away. That was another of the odd incidents Mr. Budd found so difficult to relegate to a pattern. The novelist had very obviously recognised the woman, and, just as obviously, the recognition had given him a shock. And where had she gone in the middle of the night, when Tommy Weston had followed and lost her? To see Cadell? If so, she must have reached White Cottage almost coincident with Stocking-foot.

Her signature in Mr. Ketler's register had been completely unreadable — a shapeless scrawl that might have meant anything — and she had settled her bill and gone before anyone but the landlord was up. A queer proceeding, when one took into account the way she had spent the greater part of the night. But queer proceedings seemed to be common to everybody who set foot in Chalebury.

Mr. Budd saw the melancholy Leek sitting alone in a corner of the bar; and, when he had ordered a pint of beer from the genial Mr. Ketler, the stout superintendent went over and joined him. 'Where's Weston?' he asked. 'Ain't he 'ere tonight?'

'I ain't seen 'im at all,' Leek replied. 'Not since this mornin'. Bur I've got some news fer you.'

'I hope it's good!' grunted Mr. Budd, taking a long pull at his tankard and setting it down. 'Well, get it off your chest!'

'You know those notes you found at Eales's place an' gave me ter take ter the bank an' find out who they was issued to?'

Mr. Budd nodded.

'Well, they wasn't issued ter nobody.'

'They must've bin. You mean they wasn't issued from that bank?'

'They wasn't issued ter nobody. They was forgeries! The pound notes was all right, but the two fivers was slush!'

'Slush, was they?' Mr. Budd murmured. 'Well, they was pretty good slush. They took me in.'

'The feller at the bank said there's bin a lot of 'em about durin' the last year or so. He said they're next to impossible ter tell from the real thing except by an expert. They've 'ad a lot of trouble with 'em. The whole country's been flooded with 'em.'

'Johnson!' exclaimed Mr. Budd suddenly. 'Who?'

'Johnson! You know Inspector Johnson at the Yard?'

'Oh, 'im!' said Leek. 'What's 'e got ter do with it?'

'He was tellin' me about these slush notes a month or two back. He was on the case. Hundreds an' hundreds 'ave bin put on the market, an' they can't find out who prints 'em or how they're distributed.' Mr. Budd took a gulp at his beer and went on: 'The banks were in a fever about it. Johnson said that none of the known people were responsible. The forgeries were too good, an' the paper was equal to the real stuff. He said that an entirely new bunch was at work.'

'Looks as if these notes was made by the same lot,' said Leek. 'I wonder 'ow they got inter Eales's 'ands.'

'Given to him in change, I expect. I'll send 'em up to Johnson tomorrow and see what 'e says about 'em.' Mr. Budd finished his beer and yawned. 'I think I'll go to bed,' he said, rising heavily to his feet. 'I've had a pretty tirin' day, an' maybe I'll be havin' another tomorrow.'

Which, had he but known it, was a prophetic utterance.

* * *

Immediately after breakfast, he posted the two forged notes to Inspector Johnson at Scotland Yard, from the post office in the high street, and went on to the police station. Inspector Dadds was already in his little office, though it was barely eight.

He shook his head in answer to Mr. Budd's question. 'No news at all,' he said. 'The man's completely vanished.'

'I didn't expect any,' said Mr. Budd. 'I shall be very surprised if we ever see Joe Eales again — alive, at any rate,' he added.

The inspector stroked his chin. 'It's a funny business. This place used ter be as quiet as a church. But now . . . '

'It'll get worse before it's better. The biggest sensation of all 'ull come when we find out what it's all about.'

With that, Mr. Budd took his departure. Walking up the high street, he saw a car coming towards him; and as it passed him, he caught a glimpse of the solitary figure in the driving-seat. It was the woman who had given Cadell such a shock! He turned and watched the little machine until it was out of sight, and then continued thoughtfully.

Tommy Weston was eating a belated breakfast when he got back to the inn and greeted him with a mouthful of kidney and bacon. 'Hello!' he mumbled. 'Early bird, weren't you? Did you catch your worm?'

'You're the first I've seen!' retorted Mr. Budd.

'What wit! Perhaps I should've said, did you catch your Eales? Not much difference, though, between eels and worms, is there?'

'No, I haven't found Eales . . . What have you been up to the last two or three days, Weston?'

'Me?' said Tommy, helping himself to another slice of toast.

'Yes, you! You've bin up to something, because you ain't been pesterin' me. You've bin off on yer own somewhere.'

Slowly the reporter spread butter on his toast. 'I've been prowling about the ancestral home of the Chaleburys,' he answered unexpectedly.

'An' what did you get out of that? Did you meet the Huntsman?'

Tommy shook his head. 'No, but I did hear and see something else. That business of Chalebury shooting himself in the leg bothered me. I couldn't see him as our enterprising burglar, but at the same time I couldn't stomach the explanation for the accident. So I thought I'd concentrate a bit on Chalebury, particularly after what my paper had unearthed about him. Three years ago it seems that Chalebury was as near bankruptcy as makes no difference.'

'Oh he was, was he?' murmured the big man with sudden interest.

'He'd got mixed up with a group in the City who caught him for a mug and practically took every penny he had. He got in the hands of moneylenders, mortgaged everything he owned, and generally found himself in the soup. And then, quite suddenly, he settled all his debts, paid off his mortgages, and became the gentleman of means and leisure once more. The thing is, nobody knows how it was done.'

'This is all news to me,' said Mr. Budd thoughtfully.

'A reporter's not much use if he can't give news to somebody,' remarked Tommy. 'Well, when I heard this, I began to wonder whether this sudden change mightn't have something to do with the things that had been happening round here. So the other night, when everybody had gone to bed, I strolled up to the court to have a look round. What I saw was a great deal more than I bargained for.' He drained his coffee cup and then continued: 'It was after midnight when I got to the house, and the place was in darkness except for a light in one of the upstairs windows, which I guessed to be Chalebury's bedroom. I prowled about round the grounds, kept there by some queer instinct. After about twenty minutes I became aware I wasn't the only one who was interested in Chalebury Court by night. Somebody had come up the drive in the front, and I saw him as I came round an angle of the house, looking up at the lighted window which I'd decided was Chalebury's bedroom. It was a fairly dark night, but I recognised him by his size and the coat he was wearing. It was Cadell!'

'An' what did he do?' asked the stout superintendent.

'A very queer thing,' answered the reporter slowly. 'He whistled the first three bars of 'D'ye Ken John Peel'!' He paused.

Mr. Budd, who had been slumped back in his chair, sat up with a jerk. 'Go on!' he grunted, and relapsed into his former attitude.

'After a minute or so, the window was

opened and Chalebury's head appeared. He threw something down that looked like an envelope, closed the window, and disappeared again. Cadell picked up the thing, whatever it was, and walked quickly away. That was the whole performance. I've been lurking round the court every night since, but it hasn't happened again.'

There was a long interval of silence. Mr. Budd appeared to have gone to sleep. 'A funny business!' he said at last, opening his eyes.

'That's what *I* thought,' agreed the reporter. 'I didn't know that Cadell and Chalebury were acquainted.'

'No more did anybody else. It's not generally known ... Hm, maybe it was Chalebury that brought Cadell here.'

'What do you mean?' asked Tommy, and Mr. Budd explained the mental processes that had accompanied his walk on the previous night.

'Sounds reasonable,' said Tommy approvingly. 'Yes, I should think it was Chalebury.'

'What's goin' on?' murmured Mr. Budd. 'Find that out, an' everythin' else 'ull drop into its right place.'

Mr. Ketler came in to remove the debris of Tommy Weston's breakfast, and the subject was dropped. The landlord had, as usual, an item of information to impart. 'This is a place for trouble, ain't it?' he remarked cheerfully. 'I ain't bin 'ere long, but there seems ter be always somethin' 'appening.'

'What's happened now?' asked Tommy.

'Mr. Cadell's bin attacked,' answered the landlord. 'I thought you'd 'eard.'

'Attacked?' said Mr. Budd. 'Who by?'

'Don't know who it were,' Mr. Ketler answered. 'Some tramp or other. He was comin' 'ome from a walk last night when a feller sprang at 'im in the lane near 'is 'ouse. He put up a fight, an' the feller ran away, but I'm told that Mr. Cadell got a nasty bash over the 'ead. Any'ow, 'e's in bed now.'

'How did you hear about this?' asked the reporter.

'The milkman told me. He's a rare feller fer news, is young Tilkin.'

'Apparently,' murmured Mr. Budd. 'He told you about the accident with Sir Eustace, didn't he?'

'That's right, sir,' said the beaming landlord.

'An' Mr. Cadell is in bed with a cracked head, is he?' said the big man. 'I'm very sorry to hear that. I'm so sorry that I think I'll go an' tell 'im so!' He picked up his hat, put it on, and began to struggle into his overcoat. 'P'raps you'd like to come and say how sorry you are, too, Weston?' he added as he crossed to the door.

'Yes, I'll come,' said Tommy. He had noted and wondered about the gleam in Mr. Budd's eyes. He knew nothing about the elusive memory that had been bothering the stout man, and, therefore, could not guess that it owed its presence to a sudden recollection of the circumstances in which he had met Cadell before — a recollection that had been induced by the information which the genial Mr. Ketler had just supplied.

20

The Yard Springs a Surprise

Dr. Prowse was just turning out of the drive when they reached White Cottage, and he would have passed them with a curt nod if Mr. Budd had not stopped him.

'Good mornin', doctor!' he said. 'This is very bad news about Mr. Cadell. Is he seriously hurt?'

'No; merely a slight scalp wound,' replied the old man. He looked tired, and there was an anxious expression in the faded eyes.

'Very distressin',' murmured the big man, shaking his head. 'Just one darn thing after another ... How is Sir Eustace gettin' along?'

'The wound is healing quite satisfactorily,' answered Dr. Prowse shortly. 'I'm afraid I must go. I have another patient to see.'

Mr. Budd stared after his retreating figure. 'In a hurry, wasn't he?' he remarked thoughtfully. 'Hm! I wouldn't mind bettin' that the patient he's gone to see is Miss Audrey Renton.'

'Why, is she ill?' demanded Tommy, turning a suddenly concerned face towards him.

'If she ain't, she ought to be, livin' the way she's doin'.'

'Oh, is that all?' said the reporter with relief.

'You seem to be remarkably interested,' grunted Mr. Budd.

'I am,' admitted Tommy, reddening slightly. 'I feel sorry for her.'

'I'm interested in her, too, but maybe not quite in the same way. It's my opinion she's goin' to become more interestin' still. Let's go an' see this feller Cadell.'

In response to Mr. Budd's knock, the door of White Cottage was opened by the taciturn Flecker. 'Mr. Cadell's in bed, sir,' he said when Mr. Budd asked if they could see the novelist. 'He's had an accident — '

'Hardly an accident,' interrupted the

detective. 'Tell Mr. Cadell that I should like to have a word with him, will you?'

The servant hesitated, and then with a brief request to them to wait, disappeared up the stairs. After a short delay he came back with the information that Mr. Cadell would see them.

The novelist was lying in bed propped up with pillows, his great head swathed in bandages, and he greeted them with a wry grimace. 'I've been in the wars,' he said unnecessarily. 'Sit down. What's the reason for this visit? Have you come to tell me that you've caught my burglar?'

'No, sir,' said Mr. Budd, ensconcing himself in an easy chair. 'I came to see you about this attack that was made on you last night.'

'How did you know anything about it?' Cadell demanded in astonishment.

'News travels very quickly in a place like this, sir,' replied the big man. 'How did it happen?'

'I don't know that I can tell you very much about it. The man was either a lunatic or a tramp out for what he could get. I was coming home after a walk when he sprang at me from the shadow of a hedge a few yards down the road. I was taken completely by surprise. He had some sort of a cudgel, and he gave me a nasty crack over the head before I could defend myself. It was a heavy blow, and it dazed me, but I put up a fight and the fellow cleared off. I managed to stagger as far as the house, and then I collapsed. Flecker found me and patched up my head, which was bleeding a good bit, then put me to bed. This morning we telephoned for Prowse. He came and examined me, and told me that there were no bones broken and that it was nothing serious, and a day in bed would put me right.'

'What was the fellow like?' asked Mr. Budd.

'It all happened so quickly that I saw very little of him.'

'An' I s'pose it was pretty dark, too. What build was he? Did you notice that, sir?'

'He was fairly heavily built. And as strong as a horse.'

'He didn't suggest anyone you'd seen in the village?'

'No.'

'Pity you can't give me a better description,' said the big man thoughtfully. 'I'm interested in this feller. I s'pose you don't know of any reason why someone should want to attack you?'

'If I knew of any person, I could probably put a name to my assailant,' answered Cadell. 'I don't think there was any reason other than that the man was mad, or hoping to pick up some easy money.'

'Hm, maybe,' muttered Mr. Budd dubiously. 'It's queer, though, that this feller was armed with a cudgel, an' tried to bash your head in, an' that Hicklin' an' Gowper were killed that way.'

A startled expression crossed the face of the novelist. 'Good lord! I never thought of that!'

'I thought of it d'rectly I heard you'd been attacked,' said Mr. Budd. 'I wish you'd seen more of him.'

'So that's why you're so interested in this man, eh? I rather wondered what had brought you up here so quickly . . . Well, if he did murder Hickling and Gowper, then you take my word for it that he's a homicidal maniac.'

'If he's the same man, he must be,' said Tommy Weston, nodding, 'because he had no motive for his attack on you.'

'Precisely,' agreed the novelist.

'Well, it's all very interestin' an' peculiar,' remarked Mr. Budd with a sigh. 'There's somethin' very strange an' complicated going on in this village. Are you acquainted with Sir Eustace Chalebury, sir?'

'No,' answered Cadell shortly. 'Nor have I any wish to be. Sir Eustace Chalebury is a type that I dislike intensely.'

Tommy gasped inwardly. If he had not seen that episode in the night at Chalebury Court with his own eyes, he would have been prepared to swear that the man in the bed was speaking the truth.

'Well, I can't say that I'm very partial to him meself,' remarked Mr. Budd. 'Not a very easy feller to get on with.'

'So far as I'm concerned, I have no intention of trying,' replied the novelist, and that ended the interview.

'That chap is a most consummate liar,' declared Tommy as they walked down the drive. 'Fancy saying he didn't know Chalebury! He was lying like a Trojan!'

Mr. Budd nodded absently. He was sorting out the ends of the threads which had been presented to him in such a tangle. 'An' he was whistlin' a bit o' 'John Peel' — the Huntsman's signature tune,' murmured Mr. Budd, frowning. 'Y'know, Weston, this is the queerest jumble I've ever had to unravel. There's somethin' between them two, and it isn't open an' above board, or Cadell wouldn't have to lie about knowin' Sir Eustace. The question is, has it got anythin' to do with all this other business? Is this whistlin' an' droppin' of envelopes just a little private matter between 'em, or is it connected with the murders?'

'I should say definitely yes,' answered the reporter.

'So should I,' agreed Mr. Budd. 'But what's behind it all? If we could get hold of the main thread we might be able to straighten out the tangle. But what is it, or who is it? Is it Chalebury or is it Cadell? Is it Audrey Renton, or is it the Huntsman — '

'It's certainly not Audrey Renton,' broke in Tommy emphatically.

'Don't you be too sure of that. She's in it somewhere, but whether she's the mainspring of it I don't know.'

'It's ridiculous to suggest such a thing,' said the reporter angrily.

'You think she can't do anthin' wrong just because she's pretty!' snapped Mr. Budd disgustedly. 'I tell you there's something mighty queer about that woman, Weston; I know a lot more than you do — '

'What do you know?'

'Never you mind!' said the stout superintendent rather unreasonably. 'Let's leave that alone for the moment an' see if we can get at anything by takin' events in the order of their appearance, as you might say.' Mr. Budd went through the entire catalogue of strange events and the actions of the people involved, in the order they had happened. He paused, frowned, and then concluded: 'The woman from London comes back to the inn an' clears off before anyone's about in the mornin', but she doesn't go far because I saw 'er this mornin' in her car in the high street. Audrey Renton has a visit from Dr. Prowse, an' when he leaves she puts on a pair of rubber gloves an' cuts up an' burns a suit of men's clothes.'

Tommy uttered an exclamation, but Mr. Budd made a sign for him not to interrupt. 'You see Cadell behavin' in a mysterious way during the night at Chalebury Court — whistlin' and receivin' a packet from Sir Eustace — an' Joe Eales disappears, leavin' his beer an' his money be'ind him. Two of the notes are forgeries. Cadell is attacked by a mysterious man who bashes him over the head, an' when he's asked says that he don't know Chalebury an' don't want to. That's the whole bag o' tricks, an' if you can find any sense, rhyme or reason in it you're smarter than me!'

'What's this about Audrey Renton burning clothing?' asked Tommy; and Mr. Budd told him what he had seen.

'I'll admit it's queer,' muttered the reporter.

'You surprise me,' said Mr. Budd sarcastically. 'I expected you to say it was perfectly natural.'

'I'm not quite such a fool as all that,'

snapped Tommy irritably. 'But I don't agree with you that she's mixed up with murder — '

'Well, don't let's argue about that! We need to try to reconcile all these disjointed happenin's into a coherent pattern. When that's been done, the woman's part in it 'ull be clear.'

'But you won't,' said the reporter, shaking his head. 'You won't, because you haven't got the *start* — the actual jumping-off place.'

'You mean before anything happened at all?' said Mr. Budd slowly. 'Hm! That wants some findin', Weston.'

He relapsed into silence, covering the short distance that separated them from the inn without speaking again.

Mr. Ketler was standing at the entrance, and he greeted their approach with his usual genial smile. 'There's a telegram for you, sir,' he said, addressing Mr. Budd. 'Came just after you went out.' He preceded the big man into the tap-room and went behind his bar. 'Here you are, sir.'

Mr. Budd ripped it open, read the

contents, and his face was a study.

Return at once, ran the message. *Stocking-foot arrested early this morning while attempting to break into Lord Willmot's house, Hampstead.*

It was signed by the assistant commissioner.

21

Stocking-foot

Across the pool of light that flooded his large desk, Colonel Blair surveyed the portly figure of Mr. Budd in the deep easy chair in front of him. In response to the telegram, the stout superintendent had left Chalebury by the first available train from the junction, reaching Scotland Yard shortly after seven o'clock. His heavy face looked tired, and his eyes more sleepy than usual.

'I s'pose there's no doubt that this man is Stockin'-foot, sir?' he said wearily.

'None at all,' the assistant commissioner declared. 'He's admitted to the burglaries in Hampshire last year. According to a statement he made shortly after his arrest, however, he denies all knowledge of the more recent outbreak of robberies in the shire district.'

'Do you think he was speakin' the truth, sir?'

'That, of course, is difficult to say. However, you'll be able to judge for yourself when you see the man. I've had him brought to Cannon Row. If he's telling the truth, then this fellow who's been responsible for the robberies in the Chalebury district has merely copied his methods.' The assistant commissioner opened a box on his desk and helped himself to a cigarette. 'Did you come across anything likely to lead to the identity of this other robber?'

'No, sir,' Mr. Budd sighed. 'If he ain't the original Stockin'-foot, he's just as elusive. There's a lot of funny business goin' on in that village, sir.'

'You mean the murders?'

'Them an' other things.' He hesitated, and then slowly he related all that had occurred in Chalebury since his arrival.

The assistant commissioner listened without comment until he had finished. 'A very funny business, as you say,' he remarked, frowning. 'I should think there was something pretty big behind it all. You'll be going back, of course, because your job is to find this burglar whether he's Stocking-foot or not. In finding him you may get to the bottom of the rest of it.'

'I hope so, sir,' said Mr. Budd. 'Can I go an' have a word with this feller at Cannon Row now?' Colonel Blair agreed, and the stout superintendent took his ponderous departure.

Stocking-foot, who had been brought up before the magistrate that morning and committed for trial, was a slim, youngish-looking man, neatly dressed. He had given his name as Syd Parks, and by this Mr. Budd addressed him when he was ushered into the small cell which the prisoner occupied.

'Now, Parks,' he said, 'I've seen your statement, but I want some further information.'

Parks seemed quite willing to supply him with any information that lay in his power. He answered all Mr. Budd's questions concisely and clearly. Syd Parks was his real name. He had been a clerk with a firm of ship-brokers in the City, and had been sacked because he had taken money that was not his to help pay for an operation on his wife. The firm had refrained from prosecuting but had, naturally, refused to give him a reference. His wife had died as the result of the operation and, for a long time after that, he had been out of work. Finally, hunger and desperation had forced him to turn burglar.

He had been lucky from the start. The proceeds from the series of robberies in Hampshire had enabled him to live in comfort, and to put a bit by for a rainy day. The rainy day had come. He had been taken seriously ill six weeks or so after his last coup, and had to go into hospital, where he had remained for nearly ten months. This illness had eaten up what money he had, and when he had left the hospital a week previously he had found himself destitute once more. In order to replenish his empty pockets, he had planned to burgle Lord Willmot's house at Hampstead, and here his luck had deserted him. He had been caught.

He knew nothing about the robberies at Chalebury and the neighbouring district. They had happened while he was still in hospital. The stout superintendent came away from his interview considerably puzzled.

If this man had been in hospital until a week ago, he couldn't possibly have had anything to do with the Chalebury robberies. They had been perpetrated by someone who, for reasons best known to themselves, had copied Stocking-foot's methods.

As he reached the door of his room, it opened and a man came out. 'Oh, hello, sir!' he said. 'I heard that you were back, and I thought I'd come and see you about those notes — '

'Come in, Johnson,' grunted Mr. Budd, entering the office and crossing to the padded chair behind his desk. 'Sit down.'

Inspector Johnson, a big raw-boned man with grizzled hair, put the folder he had been carrying down on the desk and hitched forward a chair.

'Now,' said Mr. Budd, digging into his waistcoat pocket and producing a cigar, 'what about them notes?'

'Well, sir,' replied the inspector, 'they're forgeries; and not only that, they're the work of the people I'm after. There's no mistaking the workmanship. It's well-nigh perfect.'

'There's bin a flood of them recently,

hasn't there?' Mr. Budd asked, lighting his cigar.

Inspector Johnson nodded. 'During the last twelve months, thousands of pounds have been put on the market. They are the most perfect forgeries that I've ever seen. The only way they've been spotted is by the numbers when they get back to the banks.'

'Hm. I s'pose the banks are kicking up a row?'

'They are! But what more can I do? None of the usual channels is being used. There's a completely new organisation at work, and my investigations have led me to a rather startling conclusion. I've got an idea that the engraver is a woman!'

'A woman, eh? What makes you think that?'

'It's a long story,' replied the inspector, 'but I'll try to cut it short. When this case was given to me, naturally the first thing I did was to check up on all the known banknote forgers, and proved to my own satisfaction that none of 'em was in this business. There was one man, however, who had been the cleverest of the lot, but unfortunately he was dead. However he had a daughter, and she was equally clever. In fact, she beat her father at engraving a copper plate. I've seen some of the designs she turned out, and they were top-notch. Although, so far as is known, she never used her talents against the law, I've been wondering if she isn't the artist at the back of this flood of slush.'

'What's her name?'

'Faith Ingram. Pretty name, isn't it? I've got her photograph here.' He opened the folder he had brought with him and took out an envelope. From this he extracted a glossy print, which he handed to Mr. Budd.

Mr. Budd looked at the picture of the pretty woman, and his face changed. The photograph was that of the one who had so startled Henry Cadell when she had arrived on that rainy night and demanded a room at the Fox and Hounds.

22

Leek's Discovery

By the light of the oil lamp in his little bedroom at the Fox and Hounds, Sergeant Leek tried to read. But the book, a battered edition of a pre-war novel he had found in the bar-parlour, was not very amusing.

His never very optimistic nature had been forced to the depths of depression by the discovery of the existence of Mr. Harry Norris and that gentleman's indisputable claim to the affections of the attractive Elsie. He felt, too, that he had made a fool of himself, and that everybody knew it. This had caused him to withdraw to the seclusion of his small room and hide his disappointment from the vulgar gaze. There was a very human streak in this melancholy man's nature.

Putting the book down with a sigh, he uncoiled his long, angular length from the bed, and, going over to the window, peered out into the darkness. The night was dry and cold. It was only nine o'clock and he had no wish to go to bed yet. Perhaps a walk would do him good.

He pulled on his shabby overcoat and hat. Turning down the lamp, he blew it out and made his way softly to the narrow staircase. The sound of voices and laughter came from the bar as he passed along the passage below and let himself out by the side entrance. The air was keen and the ground crisp as he set off briskly up the road.

For some time he walked on without any sense of the direction he was taking, and then the sight of one or two familiar landmarks woke a memory. He was unconsciously traversing the same route as he and Mr. Budd had taken on the night when they had paid their clandestine visit to Oaklands. The discovery switched his mind from his troubles to the business that had brought him to Chalebury.

Budd was interested in the gloomy house and the woman who lived in it. It was his idea that something fishy was going on there, and the woman by all accounts *was* behaving queerly. Perhaps if he had a look round he might find out something. He had nothing else to do, and it would be a feather in his cap if he could greet his superior on his return with a solution to the mystery.

He quickened his pace and presently found himself at the dark and uninviting entrance to the drive. He made sure that the torch which he always kept in his pocket was there, and stole cautiously up the weed-covered gravel. There were no lights in any of the ground-floor windows tonight. The whole house was in complete darkness.

Leek reached the clump of bushes by which he had taken up his stand before and eyed the lightless building dispiritedly. Was Audrey Renton out, or had she already gone to bed? He decided after a moment or two to make a circuit of the house, and began to pick his way carefully along the path that led to the rear portion. It was difficult going without a light, and he dared not risk even the shortest flicker of his torch. If anyone should happen to be looking out from one of those blank windows, it would be seen instantly. So he had to move gingerly, feeling his way at every step.

He came at length to a group of outbuildings and the arched entrance to a paved courtyard. A sound reached his ears from one of the buildings that loomed up vaguely in the darkness. He puzzled over it for several minutes while he stood motionless in the shadow of the house, and then it suddenly occurred to him what it was. One of the buildings comprising the small block was a stable, and the sounds he had heard were made by a horse!

He let out his pent-up breath. There was nothing to be alarmed about in a horse. He moved under the archway and looked up, but it was so very dark inside that he could see nothing clearly. He was on the point of continuing his tour of inspection when the significance of the presence of that horse struck him forcibly. The Huntsman! The ghost-rider whom he had seen with his own eyes on the first night of his arrival in Chalebury! Was this the horse that had borne him across the countryside? Had he accidentally stumbled on an important discovery? Was this gloomy house the headquarters of the Chalebury spook?

His reason told him that he was allowing his imagination to get the better of him. He was in a district where horses were common. The fact that Audrey Renton had one in her stables was not particularly surprising. It would have been surprising, really, if she had not. The fact that she seldom went out was nothing. Perhaps she did take a ride now and again for the sake of exercise. And what possible motive could she have, anyway, for masquerading as the Huntsman? Yet there was something queer about her. She had paid that money to the missing Eales, which practically proved that she had a secret she was very anxious to conceal. And there was that ring under the dead body of Gowper. It was all very bewildering; and even if she were the Huntsman, it did not make it any less so.

He moved away from the arch, skirted

the block of outbuildings, and looked up at the back of the house. In one of the top rooms a glimmer of light showed through a small window. The old woman's room, he thought. She had probably gone to bed, and so had Audrey Renton. Leek decided he was only getting very cold and wasting his time prowling about. He came back to his starting point at the clump of bushes and considered whether he should return to the inn and go to bed too, or stop where he was a little longer in case anything should happen.

The sergeant's thoughts were suddenly interrupted by the sound of an opening door, and peering across towards the porch he made out a movement at the top of the shallow flight of steps. A blot of shadow appeared against the darkness, and there was a gentle thud and the click of a closing latch. Somebody had come out of the house!

Drawing back into the shelter of the bushes, Leek strained his eyes to see who it was. As the figure moved quickly down the steps, he saw that it was a tall man, muffled in a heavy coat with up-turned collar and a soft hat pulled low over his eyes. He began to walk rapidly away down the drive, and after a moment's hesitation Leek went stealthily after him. He had no idea who the man was, but he was determined if possible to find out where he went. His destination might probably give some clue as to his identity.

In the thick blackness of the avenue it was impossible to see him, but Leek could hear him. He caught a further glimpse of him as he turned into the road, and then he lost him again in a dense patch of shadow that lay under the spreading branches of a group of trees. He waited, watching for him to come out of that shadow, but he never appeared.

The sergeant decided to risk a light at last, and, drawing his torch from his pocket, he moved stealthily to where he had last seen the man, switched on the light, and flooded the place with a white glare.

There was nobody there.

He grunted disgustedly. He must have slipped away up the road without him noticing. And yet surely he would have heard him? The next second, as he moved forward, he saw the explanation of his quarry's disappearance. Concealed by the thick trunk of a large oak tree was the entrance to a narrow lane. The man had gone this way, and while Leek had been waiting for him to reappear, must have been rapidly increasing the distance between them. It was useless to follow now.

The sergeant sighed and thrust his torch back into his pocket. The man had not been Dr. Prowse — he was sure of that. It was a much taller man — and it could scarcely have been a visitor with the whole house in darkness. Who was it?

Leek walked quickly back to the inn with this question buzzing in his brain like a fly in a jam jar, but he found no answer to it. The puzzle was, why had Audrey Renton received him in the dark?

23

A Fresh Angle

Inspector Johnson stared across the bare desk at the sleepy-eyed face of the man opposite him, the picture of astonishment. 'You saw her this morning, sir? Are you sure?'

'Quite sure,' Mr. Budd answered, lazily studying the photograph. 'This is the lady, an' you're tellin' me that she's a crook?'

'She's the *daughter* of a crook, but I've nothing against her.'

'Except that you think she's responsible for these latest forgeries,' murmured the big man thoughtfully.

'It's only an idea of mine, sir,' Johnson explained hastily. 'I've been through all the other people who'd be capable of turning out such beautiful work, and I've proved that they're not in this racket.'

'So you come to suspect this woman

— what's-her-name Ingram — by a process of elimination, eh?'

'That's about it, yes.'

'Ingram?' muttered the stout superintendent. 'Ingram. Wasn't he the feller who got four years for forgin' American dollars?'

'That's him. Charles Ingram. He served several sentences for forgery of various kinds. He died in Camberwell five years ago.'

'An' this woman's his daughter, eh? I s'pose when you started thinkin' that she was mixed up with this slush business, you tried to trace her, eh?'

'Naturally, but I couldn't find her. There was a rumour that she'd married and gone abroad, but I couldn't find any proof — '

'Married?' interrupted the big man. 'Yes, very likely. Pretty woman — talks like a lady, too.'

'The father was a very well-educated man who married a titled lady. How did you come to meet this woman, sir?'

'I've seen her twice, an' I've heard 'er talk, but I've never met 'er.' Mr. Budd gave the interested inspector an account of the circumstances in which he had seen the woman. 'An' I'm wonderin' what brought her to Chalebury.'

'Do you think it can have anything to do with these forgeries?' Johnson asked.

'Yes, I should say it was very likely. There's ghosts, an' there's blackmailers, an' there's a burglar an' a murderer in Chalebury, so why shouldn't there be a forger as well? It's only a little village, but it's just seethin' an' bubblin' with crime an' iniquity.' He drew hard at his cigar, and then went on: 'Did you ever hear of a man called Henry Cadell?'

Johnson shook his head. 'I can't recollect the name. Is he a crook?'

'He writes books, so I s'pose he is in a way. I've never read any of his, but it certainly ought to be a crim'nal offence to 'ave written some of the ones I've come across. Do you know anythin' more about this woman Ingram?'

'No, sir,' said the inspector. 'But I'd like to know quite a lot more about her.'

'It's very likely you will. I'll be goin' back to the huntin', shootin' and fishin' country termorrer, and I'll make a point of tryin' to find her. In the meanwhile, will you let me have all the information you've got about this slush?'

Johnson opened the folder he had brought with him. There were many typed reports and statements, and Mr. Budd examined them all with interest. It had started nearly a year previously. The banks, the foreign exchange offices, shops, bookmakers had all been victimised by the almost perfect forgeries. America and France had suffered equally, and the total sum involved was enormous. Somebody had netted a huge profit and was continuing to do so, for every effort of the police had failed to find the source or the distribution methods.

'The organisation's brilliant, sir,' said Inspector Johnson. 'There must be an army of agents passing these things all over the country, and yet we've never been able to get one of them.'

'There'd have to be a pretty big factory to turn out all this stuff, wouldn't there?'

'No, sir,' answered the inspector, shaking his head. 'A small electrically worked press 'ud be all that was necessary, and you could put that in a very tiny space.'

'Hm! Well, that's interestin' to know. How do they make these plates?'

'They're engraved on wax-covered copper and then immersed in a bath of acid. The acid eats into the metal where there isn't any wax. That's roughly how it's done.'

Mr. Budd wrinkled his nose. 'It must smell a bit,' he remarked. 'Nasty process, I should think. Ever bin in a large printin' works, Johnson? It's — Come in!' He broke off as there came a tap on the door, and a plainclothes man entered. 'Oh, hello, Bond. Well, what's the verdict?'

'The matron and the house-surgeon at the hospital both identify the man's photograph, sir,' replied Sergeant Bond.

Mr. Budd pursed his lips. 'So that's that! No doubt that this feller we've got is the original Stockin'-foot. All right, Bond, let me have your report later, will you?'

He dismissed the man, and after a short interval Inspector Johnson also took his departure, leaving Mr. Budd to his thoughts.

Who was the Chalebury Stocking-foot, and what was his object in copying the methods of the other? For a long time he sat thought-building, pulling down and building again. Some of the bricks fitted nicely, while others refused to fit anywhere. But with care and labour, and a lot of fresh material, it might be converted into a very trim and handsome building indeed!

★　★　★

'Give me a nice crisp, frosty mornin' any day of the week,' said Mr. Ketler, beaming jovially at Tommy Weston and Sergeant Leek as he set down the laden breakfast-tray. 'Durin' the last few wet days my rheumatics 'as been somethin' cruel.' He rubbed his right arm gingerly.

The buxom Elsie came in with the coffee, her smile rivalling the landlord's expansive grin.

'Do you suffer from rheumatics, Elsie?' asked the reporter, winking at Leek.

'No, I never 'ave nuthin' the matter with me. Why, sir?'

'I'm sure you ought to,' said Tommy. 'Standing about under damp hedges is the worst thing in the world.'

She blushed a deep scarlet, and almost ran out of the room.

'What did you mean by that?' asked Leek.

'I saw her last night, though I don't know whether she saw me. I think she was oblivious to everything except the call of romance.'

'Oh,' mumbled the sergeant. 'With that feller Norris, was she?'

'I can't say. I've never met that gentleman. Where did you go last night, anyhow?'

'How did you know I went anywhere?'

'I heard you come in.'

'I only went for a walk,' said Leek. He had no intention of telling the inquisitive reporter what he had seen at Oaklands.

The day passed without incident. Sir Eustace, according to the informative Mr. Ketler, was up again, his wound practically healed. Mr. Henry Cadell was also up again. He came into the bar at the Fox and Hounds soon after it opened that evening, and except that he was a little paler than usual, and still wore the bandage round his head, looked none the worse for his unpleasant experience. He was greeted by a chorus of respectful inquiry concerning his injury from the regular frequenters of the tap-room, and when he had answered these, carried his drink over to where Tommy Weston was sitting.

'What's the latest news?' he asked.

'Nothing's happened today, which is extraordinary. But the day isn't over yet, and — '

Before Tommy could say more, the door opened and Mr. Budd came in.

'The prodigal's return,' said the reporter as the big man joined them. 'Why didn't you wire to say when you were coming? I'd've killed the fatted calf.'

'There's bin enough killin's as it is,' said Mr. Budd. 'If you want to do any celebratin', you can buy me a pint of beer, Weston.'

'Have it with me,' put in Cadell quickly. 'What'll you have, Weston?'

Tommy suggested beer, too, and the novelist went over to the bar to order it.

'Where's that sergeant of mine?' asked Mr. Budd, looking sleepily round.

'He's in his room, I think,' answered the reporter. 'How did you get on in the big city?'

'I'll tell you presently,' grunted Mr. Budd as Cadell came back with the drinks. 'Ah, that's better!' He set the tankard down after a prodigious draught. 'Good beer, that. If women drank more of this stuff, instead of all them fancy drinks like cocktails an' such-like, it 'ud be better for 'em. An' talkin' of women, have you seen any more o' that woman what came 'ere the other night?'

Tommy saw Cadell stiffen, and shook his head. 'No,' he answered.

'I saw 'er yesterday mornin',' murmured Mr. Budd.

'Where did you see her?' broke in Cadell harshly.

'She drove past me in the high street. Nice-lookin' woman, an' a nice name, too. Faith Ingram — '

There was a tinkle of breaking glass, and Cadell, with a muttered oath, stared down at his feet.

'Slipped out of your hand, did it?' asked Mr. Budd. 'Never mind. Weston said somethin' about buying some more drinks, and — '

'Not for me, thanks,' said the novelist hastily. 'I must be going — I only dropped in for a moment.' He bade them a hurried good night and went out.

'Did you see his face?' whispered Tommy.

'You'd almost think that name had scared him, wouldn't you?' Mr. Budd said softly. 'But it wasn't the name that scared him — I'll bet that was familiar enough. It was the fact *I* knew the name that upset him.'

'Why should it?'

'Maybe he's afraid that if I know that, I may know *something else*,' remarked the big man thoughtfully.

24

The Man in the Dock

The clock in the square tower of Chalebury's little church chimed midnight, and the clear notes of the bell floated through the cold night air, reaching the ears of those few who were awake at such an hour.

Sir Eustace Chalebury, sitting morosely before the dying fire in the library at Chalebury Court, heard them and raised his eyes to check with the clock on the mantelpiece. His heavy face wore a scowl, and the sallowness of his cheeks was tinged with an unhealthy grey. He faced a difficult problem, and he could not make up his mind which was the better course to pursue. Either was dangerous. If only he had kept out of the whole thing in the beginning . . .

He stretched out a hand to the decanter that stood on the table at his elbow. He was in it — in it up to his neck — and the only thing worth thinking about was the best way out. He splashed a generous portion of whisky into a glass and gulped it down.

The clouds were gathering fast. A wise man would ensure that when the storm broke he would have adequate protection. And that was just the trouble. How could he get that protection which reason warned him would shortly be so urgently needed?

He toyed again with the idea that had gradually crept into his mind. That was a remote chance, *if* it could be worked. Unless he could hit on a plausible method of putting his plan into execution, it was likely to land him in even greater trouble. It was putting his head into the lion's mouth. But perhaps that was better than waiting for the lion to spring. It might be possible to prevent the jaws from closing if he took the initiative . . .

Henry Cadell heard the strokes of the bell as he sat in his study at White Cottage, although his thoughts were far away from Chalebury. Fragmentary pictures came bubbling up out of a sea of time, little disconnected images that flickered for a moment and were swamped. A restaurant with soft lights and the strains of a distant dance band; a dimly lighted street, with a taxi waiting before the dark entrance to an old-fashioned house; the scented darkness of a summer night in a little cottage garden; a theatre packed with people; the shimmering of moonlight on an almost placid sea. Disjointed little pictures without any kind of sequence, coming and going and coming again . . .

Faith Ingram! Had that sleepy-eyed man from Scotland Yard realised the shock he had administered when he had uttered that name? Did he know anything? And how much did he know?

Faith Ingram! More pictures from the stocked cells of his memory. The quiet room became filled with them . . .

Audrey Renton, staring into the darkness of her bedroom, heard the twelve deliberate strokes, and wondered if she would still be awake when one struck. Perhaps tonight sleep would come quicker than usual. She was tired enough. She tried to make her mind a complete blank; but thoughts would keep on crowding in, in spite of all her efforts. The fear that was always with her seemed to gather potency in the small hours. All things great and small became magnified out of their true proportion, and panic gripped her . . .

Dr. Prowse heard the bell as he made his way wearily up the stairs to his bedroom. He had had a heavy day, but his mind was not, just then, on his work. He was worried and anxious with the responsibility that weighed down his bowed shoulders. What he had done had led him into a maze of unexpected difficulties and dangers, and they seemed likely to increase. 'When once we practise to deceive . . . ' How true was the old adage!

What a tangled web he had weaved for himself! He undressed slowly with his usual methodical care, and went to bed . . .

Mr. Ketler heard the clock strike, and yawned widely and long. He was sitting at his desk in his little sitting-room at the Fox and Hounds, going through a mass of accounts, and it would be some time before his day's work would be done — another two hours at least. He yawned again and continued with his task . . .

Mr. Budd, lounging comfortably on his bed, a cigar stuck in one corner of his mouth, heard it, and the last note of the bell coincided with the end of the lugubrious Leek's recital of his adventures at Oaklands.

'Very interestin' an' peculiar,' commented the big man sleepily. 'You wouldn't be able to recognise this feller again, I s'pose?'

'I don't think I would,' said Leek. 'I never really got a good look at 'im. D'you 'ave any idea who 'e was, then?'

'Just the glimmerin' of a notion,' said his superior. 'I've got a glimmerin' of a notion about a good many things. An' you heard this horse, too. Well, well, it all fits in with what I've been thinkin'.'

'What's that?'

'It's not ready for publication yet. I've got to bring it to life.' He took the stub of the cigar from between his lips and yawned. 'I think you was a bit too quick in runnin' away. If you'd waited at that house, you might 'ave seen this mysterious feller again.'

'You think 'e'd 'ave come back?'

'I'm pretty sure he'd have *had* to come back.'

'Why?' asked the bewildered Leek.

'Why does a person usually come back to a house?' said the stout man wearily. 'Use yer common sense.'

'Well, mostly because they live there,' muttered Leek hesitantly.

'Exactly! An' that's why this feller would have come back — because 'e lives there!'

The sergeant stared at him with a frown of perplexity. 'But I thought there was only the young woman an' that old woman livin' there — ' he began.

'That's what most people think,' interrupted Mr. Budd, 'but it's my opinion that there's someone in that house nobody ever sees.'

'You mean — that 'e's bein' hid up?' gasped Leek.

'That's the conclusion I've come to, an' I believe I'm right.'

'If you are, then we've got to the bottom of all these 'ere murders and robberies an' the rest,' began Leek excitedly. 'It's obvious that this feller is at the bottom of the whole thing — '

'It's not obvious at all!' broke in Mr. Budd calmly. 'I don't think he's got anythin' to do with it!'

Leek blinked at him. 'But,' he protested feebly, 'if he ain't a crook of some sort, why's he hidin' up?'

'Ah yes, that's the point,' murmured the big man softly. 'Well, I could make a very good guess I think, but I'm not goin' to just yet.' He stubbed out the butt of his cigar in the ashtray and pursed his lips. 'I've got all sorts of half-completed bits buzzin' about in my 'ead. Ever seen one of these fellers what puts skeletons tergether? Well, I saw one once in a hospital dissectin'-room, an' I'm like that feller, only I haven't got all the bones.' He felt for another of his cigars, bit off the end, and stuck it between his teeth. 'I've got one mighty big bone, though,' he continued quietly, 'an' that's Cadell. He's a queer fish. The last time I saw him

— before we met 'im here — was in the dock at Carlboro' Street police station!'

'In the dock?' echoed the sergeant.

'Yes,' said Mr. Budd, searching for his matches. 'It's a good time ago now, gettin' on for seven or eight years. 'E didn't call himself Henry Cadell then, but I knew I'd seen him somewhere before, direc'ly I met 'im here, only I couldn't place where it was at first.'

'What was 'e doin' in the dock?'

'He was answering a charge of attemptin' to pass a forged five-pound note! He may be a well-known writer now, but 'e wasn't then! He was just an ordinary crook who'd bin caught tryin' to pass slush!'

'Was 'e found guilty?'

Mr. Budd nodded. 'This note he tried to pass wasn't just an isolated one that might have come into 'is possession by accident. He had a lot more of 'em on him, an' 'e wouldn't say how 'e got 'em. They gave him eighteen months.'

'You've got a good memory, ain't yer?'

'Not too bad,' said Mr. Budd complacently. 'An' anyway, when I remembered where I'd seen 'im before, I looked the case up! But you see what a big bone Cadell is in the buildin' up of my skeleton? He was tryin' to pass slush seven or eight years ago, an' now somebody's passin' it on a large scale. An' that's not all. He knows this woman, Faith Ingram, who came 'ere the other night, an' she's the daughter of a dead crook what specialised in slush. That's not just a coincidence.'

'But 'ow does it fit in with all the rest?'

'I'll admit that I don't know — yet. But I will. I'm goin' to have that skeleton complete down to the last little bone before I'm done, an' it won't be so long now, neither.' Mr. Budd gave a prodigious yawn. 'Now we go to bed, an' see what tomorrow will bring forth.'

But what the morrow actually brought, he was completely unprepared for.

25

Faith Ingram

The final act in the Chalebury drama began that morning. At the time there was nothing to indicate that that particular morning was in the least degree different from any other morning.

It was fine and cold. A pale yellow sun shone without heat, and a thick white frost covered fields and roads, hedges and trees. It was a morning that stirred the blood and brought colour to the cheeks.

The big man was down early and had breakfasted before Tommy Weston or the lean sergeant put in an appearance. He was feeling pleased. Out of the meagre information he had acquired, he had succeeded in constructing a plausible theory that accounted for some if not all of the events that had taken place in the vicinity of Chalebury. There were many gaps that could not be filled until further facts came his way, but at least he now knew where to look for them.

The first thing to discover was the whereabouts of Faith Ingram. That she was still somewhere in the neighbourhood, he felt sure. He went down to the little police station and put his problem to Inspector Dadds.

'It shouldn't be difficult,' Dadds said. 'If she's within a radius of fifty miles, we ought to find her before the day's out.'

'No news of Joe Eales, I s'pose?'

'None at all, sir.' The inspector shook his head. 'I should've thought we'd have found him easily.'

'I shouldn't,' retorted Mr. Budd. 'That feller's either dead, or he's been taken somewhere where nobody 'ull find him.'

'You think 'e's dead?'

'No, I don't. I'm only puttin' it forward as a possibility. But if he *is* dead, I'm wrong, an' that would be a terrible thing! I should have to reconsider all me ideas.' Before the inspector could inquire what the ideas were, he went on quickly: 'How long do you think it 'ud take you to get me a list of all the people who've come to live in Chalebury an' the surroundin' district durin' the last twelve months?'

Inspector Dadds raised his eyebrows in surprise. 'It shouldn't take very long; there aren't many strangers come to these parts.'

'I think you'll find that durin' the past year more strangers have come to live around here than ever before.'

'What makes you think that, sir?' asked Dadds in astonishment.

'Just an idea o' mine.'

'Shall I include the 'Untsman?' said the inspector with a twinkle in his eye. 'He's a newcomer, ain't he?'

Mr. Budd smiled. 'More like the oldest inhabitant! No, I don't think you need include the 'Untsman. I pretty well know all about him.'

The inspector gaped at him. 'Meanin' that you know who he is?'

'Meanin' that I *think* I know who he is,' corrected Mr. Budd.

'Who do you think 'e is, then?' said Dadds quickly.

'I think he's best described as a ghost!' answered the big man seriously.

He was gone before the bewildered inspector had time to question him further. Walking back towards the Fox and Hounds, Mr. Budd saw a small car standing outside the post office in the high street, and could scarcely believe his good fortune. It belonged to the very person he was looking for — Faith Ingram. He stopped when he drew abreast of it and waited for its owner to return.

She came after a minute or two, a trim figure in a well-cut tweed suit and a smart hat of grey felt, and would have got straight into the car with scarcely a glance at him if he had not stopped her.

'Miss Ingram, isn't it?' he murmured. She shot him a quick, suspicious look from her grey eyes — rather hard eyes, he thought.

'I think you've made a mistake — my name is Langden,' she said. 'Mrs. Langden.'

'Maybe Ingram was your maiden name?' said Mr. Budd gently. 'Your father's name was Charles Ingram, wasn't it?'

The thinnish red lips tightened. 'What right have you to question me?' she demanded.

'I've no right at all,' Mr. Budd admitted sadly. 'Only, recognising you, I thought I'd just make sure that I hadn't made a mistake.'

'How did you recognise me? I've never seen you before.'

'I've seen *you* twice before: the night you came into the Fox an' Hounds an' booked a room, an' the other mornin' in your car — '

'But how did you know my name?' she broke in. 'I signed the register at the inn in my married name.'

'You might've signed it in anybody's name! I couldn't decipher it.'

'Then — '

'I was discussin' your father at Scotland Yard, an' the feller I was discussin' him with showed me a photograph of you.' Beneath their heavy lids his eyes were watching her keenly, but she showed no sign of discomfiture.

'Oh, I see,' she said coolly. 'You're a detective, are you? Well, now that you've recognised me, and I've admitted that my name was Ingram, what then?'

'I'd just like to know what you're doin'

in Chalebury,' answered Mr. Budd. 'It interests me.'

'Does it? Well, I really don't see that it's any business of yours! Good morning!' She jerked open the door of the car and slid behind the wheel.

'One moment, ma'am,' said Mr. Budd as she pressed the starter and the engine throbbed gently. 'I'd like to have a longer talk with you sometime.'

'I don't wish to talk to *you*, now or at any time!'

'I think you will,' he answered. 'Maybe you'll have to.'

'Is that a threat?'

'No, I'm not threatenin' you, Mrs. Langden. I'm tryin' to save you a lot o' trouble, if only you knew it. Now I'm a reasonable man, an' I don't go jumpin' to conclusions like some of my friends. Maybe if someone else came an' had a talk with you, they wouldn't be so reasonable. They might just act without talkin', which is a thing I don't agree with. Where are you stayin'?'

She looked at him steadily. 'All right, I'll tell you.' She mentioned the name of a hotel in the neighbouring town. 'You can come and see me if you like, though I don't know what good it will do you.'

The car jerked forward. The superintendent stood looking after it for a second or two, and then turned into the tiny post office. There was a telephone for the convenience of customers, and he got through to Inspector Dadds after a short delay.

'Listen!' he said. 'I've just been talkin' to that woman I mentioned this morning.' He repeated the address she had given him. 'Get on to the local police an' tell 'em to put on a plainclothes man to keep an eye on her. He's not to do anythin' except keep a watch on her an' follow her wherever she goes, you understand? If she tries to leave the district, there's to be no attempt to stop her, but she mustn't be lost sight of. He's to report whatever she does, an', if possible, whoever she sees. Got that?'

The inspector signified that he had. 'Do you think it was wise lettin' her know that you were interested in her?' he ventured.

'It was the wisest thing I ever did,'

replied Mr. Budd, and then rang off. While he was paying for the call, he put a question to the elderly postmaster.

'The lady, sir?' said the old man, scratching his chin. 'She just bought a book of stamps.'

Coming out of the little shop, Mr. Budd almost bumped into Henry Cadell, who was on the point of entering. 'Good morning!' grunted the novelist. 'This is what I call real seasonable weather.'

'Very nice!' agreed the detective.

'Well,' said Cadell, as they strolled up the high street in the yellow sunlight, 'how is the investigation going on?'

'It might be better, an' it might be worse. I s'pose you haven't thought of anything that might supply a clue to the identity of the person who attacked you the other night?'

'No, I'm afraid not. I can only repeat what I suggested at the time.'

'Maybe you're right,' said Mr. Budd, 'though it 'as struck me that perhaps this feller mistook you for somebody else.'

'Not very likely. I'm a fairly conspicuous person, Superintendent!'

'Yes, I s'pose you are,' murmured Mr. Budd, surveying him sleepily. 'I've just been talkin' to that woman, Faith Ingram,' he added abruptly. 'Only she isn't callin' herself that now. She's callin' herself Mrs. Langden.'

There was a silence from the man at his side.

'What do *you* know about her?' asked Mr. Budd.

'Me?' Cadell tried to infuse a convincing note of surprise into his voice and failed lamentably. 'I know nothing about her.'

'I was watchin' you when she came into the Fox an' Hounds the other night,' said the stout man softly, 'an' you recognised her. It's no good you denyin' it. I shouldn't believe you if you did; your face gave you away.'

'I'll admit she did startle me,' muttered Cadell. 'She reminded me of — of someone I knew once.'

'I see! An' I s'pose last night when I mentioned 'er name, an' you dropped that glass — that reminded you of someone you'd once known, too!'

Cadell remained silent.

'It's no good,' continued the big man, shaking his head. 'It really ain't any good. You know this woman well enough. You recognised her when she came into the inn, not because she was like someone, but because she *was* that someone! An' you was startled last night when you found out that I knew 'er, too. Isn't that right?'

Still Cadell remained silent.

'Do you remember me tellin' you,' went on Mr. Budd relentlessly, 'soon after I saw you here, that I thought we'd met somewhere before?'

'Yes,' answered Cadell in a voice that was curiously husky. 'I said that you were mistaken, and I have no recollection of having seen you before I met you here.'

'You may not recollect seein' me, because you *didn't* see me. But *I* saw *you* — seven or maybe eight years ago. You wasn't callin' yourself Cadell then. I s'pose you took the name of Cadell when you started to write?'

'Yes.' The novelist's voice was hoarse. 'I took the name of Cadell when I started to write. It was my mother's maiden name. What's all this leading to, Superintendent?'

'It's leadin' to this,' answered Mr. Budd. 'You stated just now that you didn't know anythin' about that woman who was called Ingram an' now calls herself Langden, an' that was a lie! Langden was the name you was known by before you changed it to Cadell — an' if Faith Ingram is now Faith Langden, then she is your wife!'

26

Mr. Budd Prepares for Action

If Mr. Budd expected any sensational reaction to his accusation, he was disappointed. Cadell continued to walk on, staring straight in front of him, and it was an appreciable length of time before he spoke.

'Well?' the novelist said quietly.

'Is that all you've got to say?' demanded the big man.

'What do you expect me to say? You've just made a statement which it would be quite useless my denying.'

'Why did you pretend you didn't know this woman?'

'Is that really any business of yours?' Cadell stopped and faced Mr. Budd. 'What's your reason behind this sudden interest in my private affairs?'

Mr. Budd returned his gaze steadily. 'My interest ain't so very sudden. I've bin interested in you ever since I found you was livin' 'ere. It naturally increased when I remembered where it was I'd seen you before.'

'I see,' Cadell said very softly. 'Of course, you mean that business of the forgeries? That's where you got the name of Langden from, eh?'

'Yes,' agreed Mr. Budd. 'You got eighteen months for that, didn't you?'

'I did.'

'An' you was married then to this woman, Faith Ingram, whose father made the slush for which you was arrested?'

'Correct,' replied Cadell calmly. 'I'd been married for six months. I still don't see what all this has to do with you, though. The whole of that unfortunate business is ancient history. I served my sentence, and that was the end of it.'

'Was it the end, though? Or was it just the beginning? Durin' the past year, the market's bin flooded with slush that's so like the real thing that I'm told only an expert can tell the difference. The p'lice have bin tryin' to trace the artist an' the organisation that's distributin' it, but they haven't bin successful — up to now.'

'Only a fool could fail to realise the suggestion contained in that remark,' said Cadell, 'but my banker can give you several thousand reasons why you're mistaken.'

'Can you give me one?'

'I could if I felt inclined,' retorted the novelist. 'But I don't. If you can prove anything against me, go ahead and try! You may find yourself in serious trouble into the bargain!' He turned abruptly away and went striding rapidly up the high street.

Mr. Budd blinked after him and sighed. How foolish people were! He sighed again, and moved ponderously off to find the chief constable.

Major Hankin lived in a fine old house on the fringe of the Chalebury Estate. It had in the old days been the Dower House, and still retained its name — a mellow brick building with many gables and the tall chimneys that testified to the period in which it had been built. Mr. Budd was shown in to the chief constable's study by a neatly uniformed maid, and Hankin glanced up from a

254

document he was reading.

'Just one moment, Superintendent,' he said, 'and I'll attend to you. Sit down, will you?'

Mr. Budd sat down in the chair facing the desk and waited, filling in the time by glancing round the solidly comfortable room. Old panelling, old pictures, old furniture, old books. Nothing gimcrack and modern. The English character epitomised in one room.

Hankin finished reading the document, scrawled his signature at the bottom, and threw it into a letter-basket. 'Now, what is it, Superintendent?' he asked, leaning back in his chair.

Mr. Budd hitched forward and began to speak in his slow drawl. At almost his first words the chief constable's eyes widened, and as he went on his face expressed more and more amazement. 'You've no proof of this?' he asked when the big man finished.

'No, sir. At present it's only a theory o' mine.'

'I hardly know what to say,' Hankin declared at last. 'You're asking me to take a big responsibility — on nothing more than an idea.'

'But an idea based on certain evidence that I have been able to collect.'

'But which may be capable of a different interpretation than the one you've put on it,' the chief constable pointed out.

'In some ways, sir. I don't pretend that I know all the ins and outs of it. But fundamentally, I think I've got hold of the right end of the stick.'

At that moment there came a tap on the door and the maid entered. 'Sir Eustace Chalebury would like to see you sir,' she announced.

Hankin turned a startled face towards her, and even the sleepy-eyed Mr. Budd showed a trace of surprise.

'Good lord!' Hankin shot a quick glance at the stout superintendent. 'That's a queer coincidence. All right, Alice, show Sir Eustace into the smoking-room. Say that I'm engaged for the moment, but I'll see him in ten minutes.'

The woman departed, and the chief constable turned to Mr. Budd. 'What do you think he's come for?' he asked.

'I don't know, sir,' replied the big man, his forehead creasing, 'but I'd very much like to.'

'You haven't let him think that you suspect that — ' began Hankin uneasily, and Mr. Budd interrupted him.

'No, sir, it isn't that. Maybe it's nothing to do with this business at all.'

'Perhaps not.' Hankin pulled at his ginger moustache. 'But it's an extraordinary thing, though — just after what we'd been discussing . . . I shall have to think over what you've said. As I say, you're asking me to take on a big responsibility.'

'You'll let me know as soon as possible, won't you, sir?' said Mr. Budd. 'The men should be at their posts before dusk — '

'I'll let you know immediately after lunch,' promised Hankin.

The stout superintendent rose to take his leave. 'If this visit of Sir Eustace's should 'ave any bearin' on the matter, will you let me know?' he asked, pausing at the door.

Hankin nodded. 'When I let you know about the other matter, I'll either come or send to the Fox and Hounds.'

For a moment or two after Mr. Budd had gone, Hankin sat frowning his desk. If the big man was right, this was going to be a nasty business. There would be a terrible scandal — the sort of scandal that he, with his conservative upbringing, hated. The prestige of the county that meant much to him would suffer. All the same, he was the type of man who put duty before all else.

He rang the bell, got up and walked over to the fireplace. 'You can show Sir Eustace in now,' he said to the maid when she answered the summons, and he stood waiting in front of the blazing logs to receive his visitor.

Sir Eustace came, a grey-faced man with little of his usual bluster. 'Mornin', Hankin! I wanted to see you rather urgently.'

'Sorry I had to keep you waiting. Please sit down. Will you have a sherry or something?'

'No, thank you.' Sir Eustace dropped into a chair rather wearily. 'Don't feel too good.' There were dark puffy sacs beneath his bloodshot eyes and an unhealthy leaden hue to his skin. He looked as though he had been drinking heavily.

'What was it you wished to see me about?' Hankin asked.

Sir Eustace looked up at him, dropped his eyes, hesitated, and finally muttered: 'I wanted to ask your advice. It's rather a delicate matter. Difficult to know how to begin. The fact of the matter is — ' He stopped suddenly.

'Well, what *is* the fact of the matter?' asked Hankin. 'You don't usually beat about the bush.'

'I'm not well. I've had a lot of worry lately,' mumbled Sir Eustace, passing a trembling hand over his eyes. 'It concerns a friend of mine — I'm not going to mention any names — who's got himself in the hell of a hole. I thought perhaps you'd be able to tell me the best thing to do.'

'I might,' said Hankin, 'if I knew what the trouble was.'

'This friend of mine has been forced into something pretty serious. Some people knew something about him that would have got him into trouble if it had come out, and they used this knowledge to make him do something that he didn't want to do — understand?'

'You mean they blackmailed him?'

'That's right.' Sir Eustace nodded. 'They blackmailed him into takin' a part in a scheme that they were running. Now, what I want to know is this. Supposing this feller goes to the police and blows the gaff — will they take into consideration the fact that he was forced to do what he'd done and hush up his share in it?' He looked anxiously up at Hankin as he finished.

'It all depends,' answered the chief constable seriously. 'On the vague details you've given me, I'm afraid I can't give you a definite answer. But unless the person concerned in a blackmail case has been guilty of a very serious crime, the police are always prepared to keep his name out of the matter. But they wouldn't go so far as to condone a felony if it was serious. What was it that your, er, friend was forced to do?'

'Don't think I'd be justified in telling you that, Hankin,' said Sir Eustace. 'It's pretty serious — a criminal matter.'

'Then I'm afraid that in any statement he made to the police, he'd have to risk the consequences. He might get off lightly on account of the fact that he'd been coerced into a crime against his will, but there could be no question of guaranteeing him immunity.'

The face of the man before him paled, and his fingers went up to his mouth. 'It seems a bit unfair,' he muttered unsteadily.

'If your friend had gone to the police in the first instance, before he had allowed himself to be persuaded to take part in a criminal offence, they would have given him every help. That's really what he should have done. All he can do is to make a clean breast of it and hope for the best,' Hankin finished. He was convinced that the 'friend' was a mythical personage existing only in Sir Eustace Chalebury's imagination. What he had said referred to himself.

'Well, I'll have to pass your advice on to this feller,' muttered the baronet, getting up a little unsteadily. 'Many thanks, Hankin. You comin' to the meet tomorrow?'

'It all depends. I'm rather busy just now.'

Hankin accompanied him to the door and then went thoughtfully back to the fire. It looked as if Budd was right. A nasty business. A very nasty business indeed!

27

The Finding of Joe Eales

Mr. Budd reached the Fox and Hounds to find an angry and disconsolate Tommy Weston railing over the iniquitious stupidity of the editor, the owner, and the general administrative staff of the *Morning Wire*. 'What's bitten you?' growled the big man.

'Nothing — but I'd like to bite someone!' snapped Tommy crossly.

'Try Leek,' suggested Mr. Budd amiably. 'Take him on the mat and chew away. You won't find much meat, but — '

'Don't be funny!' interrupted the reporter. 'This is a serious matter. I've had a message recalling me to London.'

'Fine!' said Mr. Budd enthusiastically. 'When d'you go?'

'I'm supposed to catch the first available train,' replied Tommy bitterly. 'The news editor says that I'm wasting my time; that the Huntsman's a wash-out, and that Chalebury isn't supplying enough news for even a 'stick' on the back page.'

'Well, that's that!' remarked Mr. Budd with great satisfaction. 'You'll be missin' all the excitement, won't you?'

'What excitement?'

'The sensation of the century! Pity you're goin' to miss it. Well, you'll read all about it in the newspapers,' said Mr. Budd complacently. 'Not the *Wire*. *Real* newspapers!'

'Will I?' snarled Tommy. 'If there's going to be a sensation, the *Wire's* coming out first with the news!'

'There's goin' to be a sensation, all right! An' it's coming soon.'

'Can I tell the office that?' said the reporter quickly. 'Can I tell them that I've had it from you that sensational developments are expected in the Chalebury mystery? They'd let me stay on then.'

Mr. Budd considered, then: 'I think you might just mention it,' he murmured, nodding. 'Here, wait a minute!' he added sharply, as Tommy was on the point of rushing away to the nearest telephone. 'Have you got a camera? I'd like to take a few snaps — just to remind me of the place. Sort o' souvenirs.'

Tommy stared at him, suspecting that he was being facetious. 'If you really want a camera, there's one in my room. It's got a new roll of film in it, too. I won't be long.'

He hurried away. And when Sergeant Leek came drifting in later from a desultory walk, he found his superior examining the small instrument with interest. ''Allo!' said the sergeant. 'What you goin' ter do with that?'

Mr. Budd looked up. 'I'm goin' fishin',' he replied shortly.

'What do yer want a camera for to go fishin'?'

'The fish come up thinkin' they're goin' to 'ave their pictures took, and then you hook 'em!' explained Mr. Budd. 'Come outside. You're not unlike a fish yourself when you gape like that, so I can practise on you!'

Leek sighed and followed him out into the bright sunlight. For the next half-hour

Mr. Budd amused himself by using up the entire roll of film in Tommy Weston's camera. He took a picture of the inn, with Leek standing at the entrance. He took a picture of the inn with two of the villagers at the entrance. He took a picture of the genial Mr. Ketler, and another of the smiling, rosy-cheeked Elsie. He took a picture of the winding road. He took pictures of nearly everything within sight that it was possible to make a picture of; and when he had exposed the last frame he put the little camera in his pocket with a sigh of satisfaction.

'Nuthin' like a few good snaps to remind you o' the beauty of a place,' he remarked a second or two later in the tap-room, a tankard of Mr. Ketler's excellent beer in his hand. 'When I look at them pictures, I'll almost be able to taste the beer!'

'When are you thinkin' o' going back, sir?' asked the landlord.

'May be some time; may be almost at once,' he answered. 'I just 'ave to obey orders, you know.' He looked round as Tommy Weston came in. 'Well, what did your office say?'

'Quoting you did the trick,' answered the reporter. 'I'm staying.'

'Then I hope you'll make yourself useful,' said Mr. Budd.

They had barely finished lunch when Major Hankin arrived. The chief constable looked worried, but he had made up his mind to accede to Mr. Budd's request, as he quickly let the big man know when they were alone in the bar-parlour.

'I've been in communication with Leicester,' he said, 'and the men you asked for will arrive at the junction on the five-thirty-six. They'll be in the charge of Sergeant Allport, who'll take his instructions from you.'

'Thank you, sir,' murmured Mr. Budd. 'What did Sir Eustace 'ave to say?'

Hankin told him, and the stout man stroked his fleshy chin. 'Of course 'e was talkin' about himself,' he said.

'That was my opinion,' agreed the chief constable.

'I wonder if we can scare 'im into talkin'. It'd save a lot o' trouble.'

'It's hardly likely he'll convict himself.'

'Oh, I don't know. It all depends how much 'e's got the wind up. He's wonderin' what's comin' out, an' when, an' how, an' I've known people in that state do anythin' to bring matters to an 'ead.'

'It's very unpleasant,' said Hankin, shaking his head. 'A man like Chalebury! One of the oldest families in England, with centuries of tradition behind it. There'll be a tremendous scandal if you're right.'

'Two men have been killed over this business, sir,' said Mr. Budd quietly. 'I didn't know George Hicklin', an' from what I can gather, although 'e was popular, I didn't miss much. But I did know poor Gowper, an' 'e was a good feller. The only reason he died was because 'e was doin' his duty.'

The chief constable nodded. 'You're quite right,' he said. 'Anybody even remotely connected with that should not be allowed to go unpunished.'

'I'll do my best to see they don't, sir,' said the big man.

When Hankin had gone, he walked

down to the little station-house and interviewed Inspector Dadds. That official had news for him. The list of strangers who had come to live in the vicinity of Chalebury during the past twelve months was waiting. Twenty people of varying sexes and classes had taken up their residences in the neighbourhood within that period.

'An' I'll make a bet with you,' said Mr. Budd, 'that most of 'em have a criminal record. However, they ain't very important. It's the people what's using 'em that I'm after.'

'What are they bein' used for?' asked the bewildered Dadds.

'Messengers,' answered the stout man, and his reply did nothing to enlighten his questioner.

★　★　★

Mr. Budd reached the junction a bare minute before the train came in. The six men who arrived on it he carried off to the police car which had brought him from Chalebury, and during the return

269

journey he supplied Sergeant Allport with detailed instructions. It was quite dark when he returned to the Fox and Hounds a tired man, but satisfied with his labours.

'Where have you been?' demanded Tommy Weston. 'You chucked me out of the sitting-room when Hankin came, and then you disappeared. What have you been up to?'

'To use a huntin' expression,' answered Mr. Budd, 'I've bin stoppin' earths!'

Tommy gave him a disgusted look.

'You'll know all about it when the time comes, Weston.'

'But surely you can give me some idea of what you're driving at?'

'I'll do better than that. I'll show you — part of it, at any rate.'

'When?'

'Tonight! I'm goin' on a little expedition later on, an' you can come with me if you like.'

'Does a fish like water! Where are you going?'

'I'm goin' up to Oaklands,' replied Mr. Budd.

'You surely don't still think that that

270

woman's got anything to do with this business, do you?' Tommy snorted. 'I'm willing to bet anything you like that she's incapable of a criminal action! It isn't just a question of looks — '

'No, I know!' said Mr. Budd sarcastically. 'It 'ud be just the same if she had a face like an earthquake an' a figure like a barrel o' beer! I've heard all that stuff before. It's 'er beautiful soul, which you don't know nuthin' about, that makes you think butter wouldn't melt in her mouth! Bilge!'

'There's no need to be coarse,' remarked Tommy coldly. 'I've merely given you my opinion. When do we start on this excursion?'

'As soon as we've had supper,' answered Mr. Budd, and went off to his room.

It was soon after nine when they reached the dilapidated house. Tonight there were lights in the upper windows, and in the lower. But Mr. Budd was not apparently interested in the house itself, for with a whispered word to his companions he made straight towards the group of outbuildings, in one of which Leek had heard the horse moving. With great care the detective prowled around until he came to one that had a stout door, which they saw, in the momentary glimmer of his torch, had been fitted with a new and strong-looking padlock.

'Now,' murmured the stout man, 'let's see if deduction is any good.'

He took a thick piece of wire from his pocket, gave the torch to Leek to hold, and stooped down to the padlock. For nearly ten minutes he worked at it, and then there was a click, and he withdrew the padlock from the staples. A push and the door swung open into darkness.

Mr. Budd took the torch from the sergeant's hand and sent a ray of light flickering about the small whitewashed cell-like room. It came to rest on a bundle lying upon a heap of straw — a bundle that in the light was revealed as the bound and gagged figure of a man.

Mr. Budd gave a little sigh of satisfaction. 'We've found Joe Eales,' he whispered. 'I rather thought we should!'

28

The Man at the Door

Tommy Weston stared down at the huddled figure on the heap of straw in bewildered amazement. 'What's he doing here?' he whispered.

'He ain't doin' nothin',' replied Mr. Budd. 'He's unconscious.'

'But how did he get here?'

'He was brought here by your friend, Miss Renton, or by somebody workin' in her interests. Now p'r'aps you'll believe that she's capable of a criminal act?'

There was no answer to this, and being unable to find one, the reporter fell back on a question. 'How did you know he was here?'

'I didn't,' replied Mr. Budd calmly. 'But I thought it very likely he might be, and I took a chance. He might have been inside the house, but when I saw that new padlock, I guessed he was here.' He stooped over the motionless figure and peered at it. 'He's under some sort o' drug or other,' he murmured. 'Don't seem to 'ave been 'urt at all. Well, it won't do him any 'arm to stop where 'e is for a bit longer. 'E's a nasty feller, anyway.' He moved over to the door.

'What are you goin' ter do now?' asked Leek.

'I'm goin' to shut this place up as I found it, for the time bein'. I don't want to go advertisin' the fact that we've found Eales just yet, so keep as quiet as you can, will you?'

He ushered them through the doorway, closed it, and refastened the padlock. Leading the way back to the front of the house, he surveyed the lighted windows thoughtfully from the shelter of a clump of bushes. 'Queer,' he muttered. 'All this light.' He waved a hand towards the house. 'Lights in the top winders, lights in the bottom winders. I don't understand it. There's somethin' goin' on.'

'I don't — ' began the reporter, and stopped as the big man gripped his arm.

'Quiet!' he snapped. 'Listen!'

The hum of a car engine became audible. It grew louder and louder, and from the dark tunnel of the drive a light flashed. The leaves of the bushes showed greenly for a second at the bend, and then the light became two round blobs as the car turned the corner into the straight.

'Get further back!' hissed Mr. Budd, and the reporter obeyed. Crouching down among the wet shrubbery, he watched the car circle the gravelled stretch in front of the porch and stop. The door opened and a man got out quickly. Hurrying up the steps, he knocked sharply and waited. There was a slight pause, and then a light sprang up behind the transom, and the door was opened. The figure of the old woman was visible for a moment in the light that flooded out, and then the visitor stepped quickly inside, and the door was shut again.

'Did you see who that was?' murmured Mr. Budd.

'Dr. Prowse,' Tommy answered. 'Do you think Miss Renton has been taken ill?'

'Looks as though somebody has been

taken ill, don't it?' whispered the big man. 'He was in the dickens of a hurry — '

'Maybe it's the feller I saw,' put in Leek.

The reporter pricked up his ears. 'What fellow's this?'

'Never mind what feller it is,' Mr. Budd said impatiently. 'You just keep quiet and p'r'aps you'll learn a lot. There's somethin' unusual happenin' here tonight.'

Tommy checked the angry retort that rose to his lips, remembering in time that except for the stout man's intervention, he would have been back in London. It had been very good of Budd to let him in on the busines. So he waited, watching and listening, but for a long time nothing happened. The lights remained burning behind the drawn curtains, the little car with its dim headlamps stood in front of the porch, and from the house itself came an unbroken silence.

Half an hour passed slowly, and Mr. Budd stirred restlessly. 'I'm gettin' a bit too old for this sort o' job,' he said. 'We don't seem to be doin' much good here except gettin' rheumatics, so we'll try a little action for a change.' He began to walk stiffly towards the porch.

'What's the idea?' asked Tommy, following him.

'I'm goin' to join the party,' answered Mr. Budd. 'I'm tired of bein' the little boy what Santa Claus forgot! Maybe we'll be in time for a glass of sherry an' a piece o' cake!'

Mounting the steps, he gave a sharp tattoo on the knocker. There came, after a short interval, the sound of shuffling steps, and the door was opened a few inches and the old woman peered out. 'Who is it?' she demanded.

'I want to see Miss Renton,' said Mr. Budd, and, remembering his previous visit, he inserted a foot so that she could not close the door in his face.

'Miss Renton ain't in,' snapped the old woman ungraciously.

'Then I'll see Dr. Prowse,' said the big man cheerfully. 'It's no good tellin' me he ain't here, 'cause his car's still outside.'

'I ain't tellin' you nuthin'!' said the old woman, eyeing him through the narrow opening malignantly. 'Ain't you the feller what came before?'

'That's right.'

'Well, what do you want this time? Miss Renton ain't lost nothin'.'

'I want a few words with either Miss Renton or Dr. Prowse,' said Mr. Budd.

'I've told yer, Miss Renton ain't at home,' said Mrs. Willoughby, 'and Dr. Prowse is busy — '

'He can't be very busy if there's nobody in the house. Or p'r'aps he's attendin' to the drains!' Mr. Budd changed his tone suddenly. 'Listen to me, my good woman. Just you go an' tell the doctor that I want to see him, an' that I'm *goin'* ter see him, see?'

She hesitated, obviously reluctant to leave the door unguarded, and unable to close it because of his foot. She was saved the trouble of deciding, for Prowse himself appeared at that moment and demanded to know what was the matter.

'Good evenin', Doctor,' said Mr. Budd evenly. 'I wanted to see Miss Renton — '

'She's out!' broke in Dr. Prowse curtly.

'That's a pity; but p'r'aps I can talk to you instead?'

'What about?'

'Well,' said Mr. Budd slowly, 'there's quite a number of subjects I'd like to discuss with you. F'rinstance, the value of creosote as a disinfectant for drains.'

Dr. Prowse looked at him as though he had suddenly taken leave of his senses.

'I'm very interested in creosote, an' also in certain drugs that can be used safely to keep a feller unconscious.'

'I'm afraid I've no time to discuss such things!' snapped the old man impatiently.

'Then I shall have to wait an' discuss 'em with Miss Renton,' Mr. Budd remarked. 'What time will she be in?'

'You can't wait 'ere,' broke in the old woman, who had been hovering uneasily in the background. 'An' we don't know when she'll be back.'

'If you won't let me wait,' said Mr. Budd deliberately, 'I shall go away; but I shall come back with a warrant to search this house!'

Mrs. Willoughby uttered a little startled cry, and her wrinkled face went grey. The effect on Prowse was equally as suggestive. His jaw dropped, and into his eyes sprang an expression of fear. 'What for?' he muttered.

'I think you know that without me tellin' you,' said Mr. Budd gently. 'I want to know who lives in this house, apart from this woman an' Miss Renton.'

'Nobody don't live 'ere!' cried the old woman shrilly. 'Take yourself off an' — '

'Be quiet!' snapped the doctor. 'How much do you know?' he continued, eyeing the stout man uneasily.

'Everything, I think,' answered Mr. Budd.

The old man hesitated for a second, and then he made a gesture of resignation. 'Come in,' he said abruptly. He led the way across the hall to the room in which they had had their first interview with Audrey Renton. The old woman, moaning softly to herself, followed. Tommy Weston noticed the strong tarry smell that hung heavily in the air, as it had on that previous occasion.

'Is Miss Renton really out?' asked Mr. Budd when he saw that the long room was empty.

The doctor nodded.

'Where is she? It's unusual for her to be out as late as this, ain't it?'

'Very unusual,' replied Prowse. 'We don't know where she is.'

Mr. Budd's face changed suddenly. The sleepy expression vanished, and was replaced by a look of intense alertness. 'You don't know where she is?' he repeated sharply.

'No; Mrs. Willoughby says she went out this afternoon, and she hasn't come back.'

'At half-past three she went out,' put in the old woman. 'An' said she wouldn't be long.'

'Are you tellin' the truth?' snapped the big man, his face grave and anxious.

'She is,' Prowse said. 'That's what she told me when I arrived this evening. We've been rather worried.'

'You may 'ave cause to be,' said Mr. Budd grimly. ''Alf-past three — that was before my men had arrived. I didn't reckon on this, although I s'pose I ought to 'ave done. That night, when she lost her ring in Rackman's Wood — what did she see?'

'See?' The old man looked genuinely bewildered.

'She didn't tell you, then?' grunted Mr. Budd. 'She found the body of Gowper — I've guessed that for a long time — an' lost 'er ring; but she didn't say nuthin' about it because she would 'ave had to explain what she was doin' in the wood at that time o' night, an' she couldn't without givin' away the secret of this house. But what did she *see* as well?'

'I can tell you that,' broke in a deep voice from the doorway; and Mr. Budd swung round to stare in horrified surprise at the figure who stood on the threshold.

29

Henry Cadell Pays a Call

Faith Ingram pressed out the stub of her cigarette in the ashtray, drank the remains of her coffee, and rose to her feet. Crossing the almost deserted dining-room, she went out into the vestibule and made her way upstairs to her room.

She was very bored, and it was only a little after nine. But there was nothing to do except read the not very interesting novel she was halfway through, or go to bed. The Royal Hotel offered nothing in the way of amusement. There were few people staying under its dignified roof, and they were mostly middle-aged and stodgy.

She was on the point of going to bed when there came a tap on her door, and in answer to her invitation a waiter entered. 'There's a gentleman downstairs, madam,' said the man. 'He sent a message to say that he would like to see you for a few minutes.'

'Did he give any name?' she asked, frowning slightly.

'No, madam. I asked, but he said you'd know who it was.'

It must be the detective, she thought. He had said he would be coming to see her — or practically said so. 'Is he a big man?' she inquired.

The waiter nodded. 'Yes, madam.'

'Tell him that I will be down directly,' she ordered, and the man withdrew. She went over to the dressing-table, powdered her face, touched her lips with scarlet, and patted her hair.

The vestibule was empty except for the visitor, and for this she was grateful when he rose at her approach and turned toward her. 'You!' she gasped; and her face went white, so that the rouge on her cheeks showed vividly in ugly patches. 'You!'

'How long is it since we last met, Faith?' asked Henry Cadell quietly.

'A very long time.' She managed to squeeze the words out at last.

'You haven't altered much,' he said, eyeing her critically.

The first shock was passing. By an effort she steadied herself, and the colour crept back into her face. 'How did you find me?' she said, and her tone was almost normal.

'I knew you were in the district — I saw you that night you came into the Fox and Hounds,' he answered. 'I'd made up my mind not to seek you out, but . . . ' He made a gesture. ' . . . I changed my mind.'

'Why?'

'Because you're in danger. There's a detective from Scotland Yard who knows all about you — he talked to you this morning. He knows who you are, and he knows the relationship between us.'

'How does he know that?' she asked quickly. 'Did you tell him?'

'There was no need to tell him! He was present when — when I received my sentence.'

'That wasn't my fault — you know that?' she said, laying her hand on his sleeve impulsively.

He touched her fingers softly and with

almost a caress. 'I know it now,' he said gently. 'But it's taken me a long time to find out. I thought you were in it with the others. I'm afraid for a long time I was rather . . . bitter.'

'How did you discover the truth?' Faith said, almost in a whisper.

'That's too long a story to tell now,' he replied. 'I came out of prison a broken man, and I rebuilt my life under a new name. There was nothing left. Everything had gone — including you.'

'They told me that you'd died in prison. They showed me letters and papers to prove it.'

Cadell's firm mouth hardened. 'And you went abroad with Chalebury and married him! He called himself Norrington. That's why it's taken me so long to find him.'

'I only knew him as Frank Norrington,' she said. 'My father introduced me to him. I — I liked him. When they told me you were dead, he asked me to marry him, and — and I agreed. I wasn't in love with him, but everything seemed so bleak. He suggested we should be married abroad. I thought it was quite legal, until — until he told me it wasn't. He told me that just before he — he left me.'

The heavy lines of Cadell's jaw tightened, and the thick brows drew down over the deep-set eyes. 'When the time comes — and it's nearly at hand — Chalebury will pay for that!' he said quietly; and there was something in the very quietness with which he spoke that made the words all the more impressive. 'But I didn't come here tonight to talk about the past. That's over and, let's hope, done with. Faith, you're in danger. The police suspect that you're mixed up with this flood of spurious money. Knowing who you are, and who your father was, they *must* suspect you. It's only a matter of time before they act. Pack up your things and come with me while there's a chance. I don't know how deeply you're involved in this business — I don't care. If you come with me, we can be out of the country before the storm breaks. Will you?'

There was no hardness in her eyes as she slowly shook her head. 'I can't,' she said huskily. 'It's sweet and dear and generous of you, but I can't. It's too late! If you look outside, you'll probably find someone watching the entrance to this hotel.'

'How far are you implicated in this slush business?' he asked suddenly.

'I engraved the plates,' she answered. 'I didn't want to, but I had to.'

She expected him to ask why, but his thoughts seemed to be entirely concerned with her safety. 'Is there any proof of that?' he said quickly. 'I mean, could the police produce proof that you engraved the plates?'

'At the moment — no,' she answered. 'There's nothing to connect me with them at all — except my father's reputation and the fact that I *could* do them. If they found the plant, it might be different.'

'How?'

'The plant is in this district. And I'm here, too. The coincidence would take a lot of explaining away.'

'But it *could* be a coincidence. It's not proof — it'd have very little evidential value.'

'It'd go a long way with a jury, particularly with my father's record. I can't leave — not yet, anyhow.'

'Will you promise me that you won't go — alone?'

She nodded. 'Yes, I'll promise that. And I'll promise something else. If you'll ask me again — and if ever it's possible — I'll go with you.'

'It will be,' said Cadell quietly, 'and I shall ask you.'

A moment later he was gone.

★   ★   ★

Chalebury Court lay sprawling under the hard, cold sky, lightless and silent. The man who guarded the entrance to the drive wished heartily that the night was over, for he was cold and weary. His companion, ceaselessly patrolling round the house itself, was possessed of a similar wish. But a job was a job, and had to be done. Both would have welcomed some break in their monotonous task, for they had been at their posts since dusk, and nothing had happened.

Their instructions had been explicit. They were to watch the house and note everybody who called; and if Sir Eustace went out, one of them was to follow him. But nobody had called, and Sir Eustace had not left the house. It was now getting on for two o'clock in the morning, and there seemed very little likelihood that he would appear now, and even less that anyone would call. In this both the watchers were mistaken.

Just after two had struck, a man made his way stealthily through the wood that bordered the estate. He came silently, muffled to the ears in a heavy coat and wearing round his face a scarf or handkerchief that concealed his features completely. Cautiously he climbed the wire fence that divided the wood from the grounds of Chalebury Court, and crept towards the house in the shadow of a thick shrubbery.

Apparently he knew that the place was being watched, for he waited until the patrol had passed that particular point and vanished round a corner of the building before he ventured forth from his hiding-place and ran swiftly across the strip of path to the wall of the house. There was a window within his reach, and, taking something from his pocket, he worked noiselessly for a moment or two. The circle of glass he had cut out near the hasp, he pulled away attached to a piece of glued newspaper, dropped it behind a nearby bush, opened the window, and, hoisting himself through, shut it behind him. The whole operation had taken barely five minutes, and it would be another ten at least before the patrol would be round again.

In the darkness of the little room in which he found himself, the night visitor proceeded to draw woollen stockings over his shoes, and when he had done this, he moved silently out into the great hall. A tiny thread of light no bigger than a thick string came from the torch he carried, and guided his feet up the big staircase. He paused on the first landing, found the corridor he was seeking, and crept along it until he came to the door of Sir Eustace Chalebury's bedroom. Again he paused, listened, put the torch in his pocket, and tried the handle of the door. It was locked as he had expected, but he had come provided for such an emergency, and after a few seconds' work on the lock, the door opened under his hand and he slid silently into the room.

The heavy breathing of the occupant came to his ears, and his lips curled beneath the mask. Sir Eustace had wooed sleep from the whisky bottle. The air was full of the fumes of stale drink. Well, so much the better.

The muffled figure moved towards the bed, drawing from its breast pocket a long-bladed knife. A gloved hand went searching for the sleeper, and the knife was raised.

30

The Secret of Oaklands

At the unexpected sound of that deep voice, Mrs. Willoughby gave a little whimpering cry, and her bony hands went up to the bosom of her black gown. Dr. Prowse made no sound, but the muscles of his face tightened and his hands clenched until the knuckles showed milk-white through the stretched skin. For a moment there was an utter silence, and then Mr. Budd spoke.

'Mr. Andrew Renton, I think?' he said softly.

'You think rightly,' he answered. 'I am Andrew Renton, or all that remains of him.'

'Andrew! Why did you come down?' exclaimed the old man hoarsely. 'Why did you want to show yourself — '

'Because I am tired of all this secrecy,' broke in Renton impatiently. 'Look what it's led to. Audrey has spent the whole time in a state of constant worry and anxiety, which has had a bad effect on her health, and now she's in danger of her life! I should never have agreed to the scheme in the first place. It was thoughtless and self-ish. I ought to have resigned myself to the inevitable. Anyway, my appearance doesn't seem to have been so very unexpected.' He turned his dreadful face towards Mr. Budd.

The detective shook his head. 'It wasn't, sir,' he said. 'I knew you was here, an' I knew *why* you was here!'

'How did you know?' rasped Dr. Prowse. 'How *could* you know?'

'I s'pose you'd call it a matter o' deduction an' elim'nation,' Mr. Budd replied. 'It wasn't very difficult, really. Miss Renton livin' here all alone an' never goin' out like other gals of her age wasn't natural to begin with. Even the fact that she was s'posed to be grievin' over her father's death didn't seem a sufficient reason to my way o' thinkin' for livin' in a big house without any proper servants. An' then there was the state of the place. Surely, however cut up she was, it wouldn't have done any 'arm to have kept the house an' the garden in a decent condition? She had the money, so it wasn't that. I heard all about her from Major Hankin on the day I found that ring, an' it sounded queer to me. It seemed queerer when I called. The house was reekin' with a tarry smell, which she explained by sayin' she'd bin puttin' creosote down the drains. But it wasn't creosote that was makin' the smell.

'I got a bullet in me thigh some years ago, an' I 'ad to have an operation. The 'ospital where I went was full of the same smell, an' I recognised it. It set me thinkin', particularly when I took it in conjunction with her manner. She was scared of somethin' — I could see that in her eyes — an' I wasn't satisfied over her explanation of how she had lost her ring. Then I found that the doctor here was a frequent visitor, an' one night when I was prowlin' round I saw him leave. The same night after 'e'd gone, I 'ad a peek through the window, an' I saw a very queer thing. Miss Renton was burnin' a man's clothes in the fire, an' she was 'andlin' 'em with rubber gloves!

'After that, I began to put two an' two together. A house that reeked with a strong disinfectant, no servants except a woman who 'ad bin 'er old nurse, the only visitor a doctor who was also an old friend, an' this burnin' clothes wearin' rubber gloves. It seemed to me pretty certain that all this added up to the fact that there was someone in the house who was ill an' someone whose presence there, an' the fact that they was ill, had to be kept secret. The more I thought about it, the surer I became that if there was such a person, it could only be her father. He was s'posed to have died in Africa — but had 'e? S'posin' 'e'd contracted some infectious disease an' she was hidin' him up an' attendin' to him sooner than he should have to go to an isolation 'ospital? But I still couldn't see why there was any need for all this secrecy unless 'e'd done somethin' against the law. An' then I remembered what Joe Eales 'ad told me about the Huntsman. He'd seen him quite close one night, an' he described him. I knew then. The disease was leprosy!'

Tommy Weston, who in company with Leek had been watching and listening in breathless amazement, uttered a quickly stifled gasp of horror. So that was the explanation for the mottled silver-grey face of the man in the doorway? Andrew Renton was a leper!

'You are quite right.' The deep voice came calmly, but tinged with a tragic despair. 'I contracted this loathsome thing in an unknown part of South Africa. The disease is not uncommon out there. At first the signs were slight, and I hoped that it might prove to be only ichthyosis, a skin disease like leprosy, but curable and comparatively harmless. I came to England in a fruit boat, and was met by my old friend, Prowse.

'He examined me and pronounced my death sentence. I was horrified. If it was known, the authorities would insist that I should be instantly removed to a leper hospital. I had to have time to think what was best to be done in the awful circumstances in which Fate had placed me. At my request, Prowse notified my daughter, and in company with Mrs. Willoughby she came to see me. We discussed the whole dreadful situation, and she wouldn't hear of anything being made public. She suggested that the servants should be dismissed, that it should be given out that I had died abroad, and that I should come back and live in secret in my own house, looked after by Mrs. Willoughby, herself, and Prowse. It was a temptation to which I regret that I succumbed. But, although Prowse warned me that it was impossible, I had in those days a desperate hope that I could be cured.'

'An' of course, you was the Huntsman, sir?' said Mr. Budd.

'I was the Huntsman,' answered Renton. 'I had to have exercise, and I used to take walks by night. But I had been used to riding, and I longed to get astride a horse. The legend of the Chalebury family offered me an opportunity. I knew that if I was seen by any of the villagers, I should not be inquired into too closely.'

'I guessed that was the explanation

when I'd figured out the rest,' said Mr. Budd. 'I s'pose Eales discovered who you were an' put the black on Miss Renton?'

'He overheard us talking one night,' replied Renton. 'My daughter had been out with me for a walk — I gave up the ghost business when you arrived in the village, because I didn't want to risk being caught — and we must have passed Eales while he was at his poaching. Anyway, he knew all about me, and he demanded payment to keep quiet.'

'An' you decided he should disappear.'

'I was responsible for that,' put in Dr. Prowse quickly. 'I knew Eales, and I foresaw that he would go on demanding money forever unless he was stopped. I called on him, drugged him with a hypodermic syringe, and brought him here. He lashed out and made my nose bleed before he lost consciousness, though,' he added, tenderly stroking his thin nose.

'Well, you seem to have broken all the laws you could,' said Mr. Budd sternly. 'What were you goin' ter do with this feller?'

'Make him go abroad with a lump

sum,' answered Renton. 'I knew the skipper of a cargo-boat who would have dumped him on one of the South Sea Islands, and asked no questions, if he'd had a note from me.'

'An' you think he'd 'ave stopped there?' said the superintendent doubtfully. 'Hm. You'd have had him back by the — '

'Look here!' interrupted Tommy Weston suddenly. 'Don't you think we'd better go into all this later? Isn't it more important at the moment that we should find out what's happened to Miss Renton than stand here wasting time talking?'

'You're right for once, Weston,' said Mr. Budd. He turned swiftly towards Renton. 'You were goin' to tell me what it was your daughter saw that night when she lost her ring?'

'She saw the man who killed Gowper!' answered the explorer.

'She saw the murderer?' snapped Mr. Budd, and his sleepy eyes opened with a jerk. 'Who did she see?'

'I don't know.' Renton shook his head. 'She was out with me. We'd been for a walk, and were coming home through

Rackman's Wood when I caught my foot in the root of a tree and twisted my ankle. It was a nasty wrench, and painful. I had to lean against a tree, and I suggested that Audrey should go on home and that I would follow as soon as I could walk. She was tired, and after a little persuasion she agreed.

'I was just beginning to hobble when she came running back and told me that she'd reached the edge of the wood when a man had started up out of the undergrowth and taken to his heels. She thought at first that he was a poacher, and had gone to see what he'd been doing, expecting to find a snare. She found instead the dead body of a man. She was terrified, as well she might be.

'It took me some time to reach the spot in my crippled condition, and then I found — Gowper. He was quite dead — his head was in a dreadful state — and there was nothing to be done. We decided to say nothing. It would have meant Audrey explaining what she'd been doing in the wood at that time of night, and that would have been difficult. When we got back here, she found that she'd lost her ring — '

'An' did she recognise this man who ran away?' broke in Mr. Budd.

'I think she did,' replied Renton seriously. 'She never actually said so, but I'm sure she did.'

'Must we go on talking?' said Tommy impatiently. 'Can't we be doing something — '

'We'll do somethin' when there's somethin' to be done,' snarled Mr. Budd. 'Where was Miss Renton goin' when she left here this afternoon at half-past three?' He swung round and snapped the question at the old woman.

'I don't know!' whimpered Mrs. Willoughby. 'She just said she was goin' out — '

'If this man knew she had recognised him,' broke in the reporter, 'heaven knows what may have happened to her! It's criminal to waste any more time — '

'What do you suggest doin'?' said Mr. Budd. 'Runnin' round in circles? Keep quiet for a moment an' let me think, will you?'

'That's all very well,' said Tommy stubbornly, 'but don't you realise she may be in the greatest danger? Good God, she went out at half-past three and it's now half-past eleven!'

'I can't move yet!' said Mr. Budd. 'If I move too soon, he may slip through me fingers altogether.'

'I don't care a hoot about anything except Miss Renton's safety!' cried Tommy, and his face was haggard with anxiety. 'We've got to find her!'

'I'm thinkin' about her safety, too!' snarled the detective irritably. 'Only, I'm tryin' to think sensibly. It's no good rushin' things.'

'Have you any idea who this man is?' asked Renton.

To Tommy's surprise, Mr. Budd nodded. 'I've a very good idea.'

'Then for God's sake, what are you waiting for?' exclaimed the reporter. 'Why don't you go and pull him in?'

'Because I've no proof! You can't arrest a man on an idea!'

'And while you're waiting for proof, what happens to Miss Renton?'

'That's what's worryin' me,' admitted the superintendent, frowning heavily.

'Do you really think my daughter's in danger?' asked Renton anxiously.

'Well,' said Mr. Budd, 'there's no disguisin' the fact that if she recognised the criminal on the night Gowper was killed, she'd be a source of danger to him. The question is, does he *know* she recognised him?'

'The only question that is of the least importance,' said Tommy, 'is where is she?'

He had scarcely finished speaking when the answer came. The sound of stumbling footsteps reached their ears from the drive outside, followed almost at once by a jerky, impatient knocking on the front door.

'Who can that be?' muttered Renton. 'You'd better see, Mrs. Willoughby.'

The old woman was moving towards the door when Mr. Budd stopped her. 'I'll see,' he said curtly. 'Take Mr. Renton back upstairs, Doctor.'

The knocking was repeated as the doctor and his patient disappeared into the hall; and, giving them time to get out of sight up the staircase, the superintendent opened the front door. Audrey Renton almost fell into his arms!

31

Audrey Renton's Story

The woman was exhausted and dishevelled. Her neat tweed costume was crumpled and torn, and she was covered in mud from head to foot. Mr. Budd slid an arm round her as she stood panting and swaying in the dimly lighted hall. 'Come along in an' sit down, m'dear,' he said kindly. 'You seem to have had a rough time.'

She looked at him dazedly and allowed herself to be led into the long room. Mrs. Willoughby gave a squeal of concern as she saw the condition of her mistress, and began to fuss round her like an ancient and scraggy hen.

'Get her some tea, or somethin',' said Mr. Budd as Audrey was deposited in a chair, 'an' leave her alone. All she wants is time to recover. There's nuthin' much the matter with 'er.'

'What happened? How did she get in this state?' asked Tommy, hovering anxiously around.

Mr. Budd gave him a withering glance. 'What d'you think I am — a thought reader?' he demanded. 'Maybe she'll tell us when she's rested a bit.'

Audrey was recovering. Her eyes were losing their dazed expression, and she was glancing uneasily from one to the other of them. 'What — what are you all doing here?' she muttered, raising a shaking hand and brushing the straggling hair back from her forehead.

'Now don't you go worryin', miss,' said Mr. Budd gently. 'You just take it easy. The old lady's gone to make you a nice cup o' tea. You'll feel better when you've had that.'

'I feel all right.' She tried to sit up but sank back. 'Why are you here? What are you doing in this house?'

Mr. Budd carefully evaded a direct reply. It would be unwise to inflict a further shock just then. Better to wait until she had completely recovered before letting her know that the secret she had been at such pains to guard was a secret no longer. 'Just you rest yourself,' he said soothingly, 'an' presently you can tell us what happened.'

Her forehead puckered in a frown, and she looked perplexed and uneasy. Their presence in the house was unexpected, and it obviously worried her. An awkward silence was broken by the arrival of Mrs. Willoughby with tea.

'Here you are, dearie,' she said. 'Just you drink this, an' you'll feel right as rain.'

Audrey took the cup and saucer and sipped the hot tea gratefully. By the time she had finished it, although still white and shaken, she was looking more normal.

'Now, miss,' said Mr. Budd, 'if you feel strong enough, p'raps you'll explain how you came to get in this state.'

She looked at him a little resentfully. 'I don't know by what right you should question me,' she began, 'or why — '

'Let's forget all that,' he interrupted with a gesture of impatience. 'I know how you feel, miss, an' what you're thinkin'.

You're thinkin' that you can't explain without givin' away somethin' that you don't want me to know. Well, you needn't worry about that. I do know! That's why I'm here.'

She stared at him apprehensively, her wide eyes filled with fear. 'You know?' she whispered. 'What do you know?'

'Everything,' he replied. 'But you needn't be afraid. I'm not concerned with the rights or wrongs of what you've done. The only thin' that concerns me is the fact that you've bin concealin' evidence that would've helped to bring a murderer to justice. That's a serious offence, miss; in law, it makes you an accessory after the fact.'

'I don't know what you mean,' she muttered.

'It's no good, miss,' said Mr. Budd, shaking his head slowly. 'I've told you that I know, an' that's the truth. Just before you arrived, I was speakin' to your father — '

'My father!' She was on her feet, white-faced and trembling. The old woman hurried to her side, but she waved her away. 'My father!' she repeated.

'Yes, miss,' Mr. Budd said gently. 'Sit down an' don't get upset. I've seen your father an' Dr. Prowse — the doctor's upstairs with him now.'

She looked at him dully, and from him to the old woman.

'That's right, dearie,' mumbled Mrs. Willoughby in reply to the mute question. 'The master came down while they was here.'

'So you see, miss,' went on Mr. Budd, 'there's no reason for any more hidin' up.'

Audrey sank back into her chair. 'What do you want to know?' she asked in a voice that held such a note of hopelessness in it that Tommy Weston felt an unusual tug at his heartstrings.

'I want to know what 'appened this afternoon,' said Mr. Budd. 'You went out at half-past three, an' you've just come back. You didn't stay away of your own accord. What happened?'

She moistened her lips, but she did not speak.

'On the night Gowper was killed, you saw somebody in Rackman's Wood, didn't you?' prompted Mr. Budd. 'An' you recognised 'im.'

She nodded.

'But, although you guessed that he was the man who had killed Gowper, you said nothing — not even to your father?'

'I said nothing to anybody,' answered Audrey. 'I — I dared not say anything. He — he knew I had seen him, and he knew about — about Father. He said that if I gave him away, he'd give *me* away.'

'When did he say this?'

'I met him the day after — while I was out for a walk — and he stopped me.' She gave a little shudder. 'It — it's been a nightmare, knowing and not being able to speak.'

'It might 'ave bin even worse,' said Mr. Budd gravely. 'You were a danger to this man's safety, an' he's a killer. I think you're very lucky, miss, to be still alive, knowing what you know.'

'He knew I wouldn't — couldn't give him away,' she replied. 'I met him again — this afternoon — by accident, in the little lane that runs down to the village. He attacked me, and I don't remember any more until I found myself lying in the dark, gagged and bound. I was desperately frightened. I didn't know what had happened, or where I was; but I realised that I was in danger. I managed after hours and hours of struggling to free myself, and discovered that I had been taken to a disused keeper's hut on the Chalebury estate. I ran all the way here,' she finished her jerky narrative breathlessly.

'And you were lucky to have got away,' said Mr. Budd very seriously. 'I wouldn't mind bettin' that he was only keepin' you there until he had time to finish the job properly.' He pursed his lips. 'He's got the wind up,' he went on thoughtfully. 'That's obvious, or he wouldn't 'ave tried this. He's coverin' his tracks, an' you were a potential danger. A witness who could identify him. While there was no likelihood of your secret comin' to light, he didn't bother about you. He knew that you wouldn't say anythin' while you were tryin' to keep your father's secret; but once *that* was known, you'd speak. That accidental meetin' with you this afternoon, in that lonely lane, must 'ave seemed to 'im like an act o' Providence.'

'Who is this man?' demanded Tommy.

'He's the feller behind the whole business,' answered Mr. Budd. 'He's the feller who killed Hicklin' an' Gowper. Without 'im there would've bin no Chalebury mystery.'

'But *who* is he?' asked the reporter impatiently.

The big man looked at him sleepily. 'You'll know before mornin',' he replied. 'I needn't hold me hand any longer, now. I was waitin' to get proof, but Miss Renton's the best proof I could've got. She can identify 'im. She's the one witness I've bin waitin' for.'

He glanced at his watch. 'Ten minutes past twelve,' he said. 'I think we'd better be goin'.' He looked at Audrey's pale, wan face. 'If you take my advice, miss,' he added kindly, 'you'll get off to bed an' have a good sleep. By the time you wake, it'll all be over.'

They were to remember his words before dawn broke, for he spoke prophetically. Before the sun came up it *was* all over, though in a different way to that which any of them expected.

313

Andrew Renton paced up and down the sitting-room of his isolated suite at the top of the house. The whole of the upper floor had been shut off from the rest of the building by a thick partition, in which was set a door that was kept locked. In this virtual prison he had spent the last twelve months of his life, for Dr. Prowse had ruled that except during those periods when he went abroad for exercise, total isolation was essential for the safety of the rest of the household.

Here in an atmosphere that reeked of disinfectants, he lived and had his being — and, so long as the precautions Prowse had laid down were rigidly adhered to, safe in the knowledge that there was no risk of passing on the dread disease from which he suffered. He had become resigned to the fact that there was no cure, although at first this had been his constant hope — resigned to this death in life that had reduced him from a happy, active man to a hermit, cut off forever from communicating with the outside world.

And now even this retreat would shortly be taken from him. The authorities, now that his secret was known, would act speedily. He had been a weak fool to listen in the first place to the pleadings of his daughter; he should have faced the situation and refused to agree. But it would have meant isolation in a strange place, without friends and without the daughter whom he loved; and there had until recently always been that desperate hope that he could be cured.

More than once of late he had contemplated suicide. Death seemed preferable to this terrible wasting away. And death would release Audrey from her self-imposed sacrifice.

He was thankful that she was back safe and sound. He had seen her for a moment before she went to bed, and learned of her experience at the hands of the man who had killed Gowper. And indirectly, he himself was responsible. But for him, she would never have been in the wood that night — never been subjected to the ordeal her presence there had brought about.

Up and down the room he went in a

ceaseless patrol. Audrey and Mrs. Willoughby were sleeping, or at least in bed; but the excitement of the evening had left him restless. Presently a kind of claustrophobia came over him. The room seemed to be closing in on him, and he longed for space and air. An intense desire for a gallop across the wide, clean-smelling country took possession of him — a desire to get on the back of a horse and ride and ride and ride. Well, why not? There was no reason not to, now. He could have a last ride before they removed him to a place where riding would be impossible.

For the last time, the Huntsman should appear in Chalebury.

Rapidly he took out of a wardrobe the pink coat, the riding breeches, and the rest of the habiliments, and put them on. Taking the key to the stables from a drawer, he made his way silently through the sleeping house and let himself out by the back door.

The big black horse was pleased to see him, and whinnied softly. He patted its head with his gloved hand, and in the light of the hurricane lantern, which he had brought from the kitchen, found saddle and bridle. He led the animal gently out and down the drive to the road, and, mounting, cantered away at a brisk trot, humming softly the strains of 'John Peel' . . .

32

The Hunt

Mr. Budd put back the telephone receiver and looked across at the sleepy-eyed Inspector Dadds. 'The chief constable'll be here in a few minutes,' he said. 'Didn't sound too pleased, though, at bein' woke up.'

The inspector grunted. He rather sympathised with the chief constable. He had not been too pleased at being woke up himself. 'Wouldn't it have been best to wait until the morning?' he ventured, stifling a yawn.

'No, it wouldn't!' retorted Mr. Budd. 'Circumstances alter cases, an' I'm goin' to take this feller tonight.' He felt in the pocket of his waistcoat for one of his cigars, found that there were none left, and sighed.

Tommy Weston, perched on the corner of the desk in the little office, eyed him

318

speculatively. 'Why don't you tell us who this man is?' he demanded for the umpteenth time since they had left Oaklands.

'Why don't you stop bein' impatient?' growled the superintendent. 'You'll know all about it if you wait.'

The reporter made a gesture of irritation. He had received the same reply to all his questions. When they had left Audrey Renton's house, he had expected that they would return to the inn; but it was soon evident that Mr. Budd had no such intention. He had taken Sergeant Leek aside and sent that melancholy man off on some errand, the nature of which he refused to divulge; and, still maintaining a stolid silence that all Tommy's threats and pleadings failed to break, had made his way as rapidly as his physique would allow to the police station. Here he had sent for Inspector Dadds, and when that man had arrived, a little aggrieved at having his rest disturbed, he had merely remarked that they had a busy night before them, and continued his policy of saying nothing. Both Tommy and the inspector were naturally resentful of this attitude, but the superintendent remained completely unperturbed.

'This isn't the time for talkin',' he said in reply to a question from the local man. 'Tonight's goin' to see the end of this business, an' when it's over you can answer all the questions yourself.' And with that Dadds had to be content.

'If you're going to take this man, whoever he is,' said Tommy after a moment's silence, 'why don't you do it? What are we waiting here for?'

'We're waitin' for Major Hankin,' replied Mr. Budd. 'This has got to be done properly, accordin' to the rules an' regulations. You might liken this to a sort o' 'meet', if you've got that kind of imagination. We're waitin' until all the 'untsmen an' the 'ounds is ready, an' then we'll go an' draw the covert.'

Tommy snorted disgustedly. 'Very poetical!' he said wrathfully. 'I hope you're not cheated of your kill.'

'I don't think you need worry about that,' said Mr. Budd complacently. 'I've stopped all the earths, I think.'

The reporter looked helplessly at Dadds, and the inspector shrugged his shoulders. 'It's sheer cussedness!' declared Tommy. 'There's no reason why you shouldn't tell us who this man is you're after, is there?'

'No reason at all!' answered Mr. Budd blandly. 'Except that I'm not goin' to! I don't believe in wastin' breath in repeatin' meself. Maybe when Major Hankin gets 'ere, your curiosity 'ull be satisfied.'

'I see. Just pure laziness, eh?'

'Method!' corrected Mr. Budd. 'Method, Weston. I don't believe in doin' a job twice, if I can avoid it.'

It seemed to the impatient and curious reporter that the chief constable was an age before he put in an appearance. In reality he reached the little station-house barely fifteen minutes after Mr. Budd had put through the call. He came in quickly, showing signs of the rapidity with which he had dressed.

'What is it, Superintendent?' he asked without preliminary. 'You said the matter was urgent.'

Mr. Budd became suddenly very alert and businesslike. 'It is, sir,' he answered.

'I'm taking the man responsible for the murders of Gowper an' Hicklin' tonight — within the next hour an' a half, I hope.'

Hankin's shaggy ginger brows shot up. 'You know him?' he exclaimed.

'I've guessed him for quite a while, sir. A few hours ago I got proof. Did you bring that blank warrant?'

The chief constable nodded and tapped his breast pocket. 'I got it signed yesterday as you requested. No name has been filled in — '

'I'll fill in the name,' interrupted Mr. Budd. 'I'm glad you got it. I thought we might 'ave to act quickly.'

'Who is this man?' asked Hankin.

'I'll come to his name in a minute or two. There's somethin' I want to tell you first.' He began, before the chief constable had time to put any further question, to relate, briefly and clearly, exactly what they had discovered at Oaklands earlier that night. Hankin listened, his astonishment growing visibly as the superintendent proceeded.

'Good heavens!' he exclaimed when Mr. Budd had finished. 'It's incredible! I never guessed for a moment that Andrew Renton was alive.'

'I don't think anyone guessed, sir,' said Mr. Budd, 'except me.'

'No wonder that poor woman always looked so ill and worried. What a terrible responsibility — what a dreadful burden!'

'I think the worst burden was knowing this murderer an' bein' afraid to tell,' murmured Mr. Budd. 'She had to bear that alone. She never said anythin' about that to her father, or to Dr. Prowse, or to the old nurse.'

'And she nearly lost her life over it. Who is this man, Budd?'

'Give me that warrant, sir,' answered the superintendent, 'an' I'll fill in the name.'

Hankin put his hand into his breast pocket and produced the document. Spreading it out on the desk in front of him, Mr. Budd picked up a pen, found the place with a forefinger where the name had to be inserted, and wrote laboriously. They crowded him, staring with startled, incredulous eyes as the letters formed slowly beneath his hand.

'It's impossible — quite impossible!'

breathed the chief constable. 'You must've made a mistake.'

'I haven't, sir,' said Mr. Budd, shaking his head. 'That's the man who killed Gowper an' Hicklin', an' was responsible for these Stockin'-foot robberies. I don't s'pose that's his real name — we'll most likely find that out later — but that's the name we know 'im by, an' it's good enough for our purpose.'

Tommy Weston was still staring speechlessly at the name the detective had written. 'I should never even have suspected him,' he gasped.

'No more should I,' said Mr. Budd, 'if it hadn't been for one thing.'

'What was that?' demanded the reporter.

'That piece o' paper that he used to stuff in the torch which he left behind at Cadell's. An' I didn't realise the significance o' that until an accident showed me. Then I did. But suspicion an' proof are two very different fish. I was waitin' to get proof before I moved, an' now Miss Renton's supplied it.'

He rose to his feet heavily. 'We may as well get goin',' he said. 'It's nearly half-past one, an' we'd better not leave it any later. You understand now why I couldn't leave it till the mornin'?'

Apparently they did not, for they only surveyed him in silence.

'I should've thought it was easy,' murmured Mr. Budd. 'He might've gone back to the place where he left Miss Renton to complete his job, an' found she was gone. He'd know then that the game was up.'

'He may have done that already,' exclaimed Tommy.

Mr. Budd shook his head. 'If he had, I should've known it. I've had two men watchin' the house ever since dusk. If he'd left it, I'd've been notified.'

He was halfway to the door when from the silent street outside came the sound of running, uneven, stumbling footsteps, as though the runner were well nigh exhausted.

'Who can that be — ' began Hankin; but Mr. Budd was already out of the office and lumbering across the tiny charge-room. A thin figure came staggering unsteadily into the police station as he reached the entrance. It was Leek!

'He's gone!' gasped the sergeant painfully. 'He's gone! I've run all the way ter tell yer . . . ' His breath gave out and he panted jerkily like a newly landed fish, his hand pressed to his side.

'What d'you mean, gone?' snapped his superior. 'How could he have gone with those two men watching the place?'

'He must 'ave dodged 'em somehow,' stammered Leek between great gulping breaths. 'He's gone, anyway.'

Mr. Budd swung round towards the chief constable. 'You've got your car here, sir, haven't you?' he said harshly, and Hankin nodded. 'Those two nitwits have let the fox break cover! Come on — we've got to go after him in full cry, an' hope the scent's a strong one!'

He hurried out of the station-house and pulled open the door of Hankin's car. 'Wonderful how quickly you pick up these huntin' expressions, ain't it?' he remarked as the other tumbled in beside him. 'Still, they're appropriate to the occasion. As fast as you can, sir. We haven't any time to lose,' he added, and the car shot away down the deserted country road.

33

The Kill!

In Sir Eustace Chalebury's darkened bedroom at Chalebury Court, the man who had come like a shadow to the house stood motionless beside the bed. There was no sound of heavy breathing now — nothing but complete and absolute silence.

The murderer's lips twisted into a mirthless grin as he stooped and wiped the knife on the coverlet. The man who had contemplated squealing would have to squeal very loudly now to be heard — so loudly that his voice would reach from hell.

He put away the knife and left the silent thing on the bed, moving out into the centre of the room. There was only the woman, now, and he would be safe. He could deal with her before he returned. The men who were watching him had not seen him leave, and they would not see him return. There was a way by which he could come and go that was unsuspected. Instead of being a danger to his safety, those men would, all unwittingly, provide him with a cast-iron alibi; for what better alibi could a man have than the evidence of the police themselves?

Again he grinned to himself in the darkness. In some way or other the fat detective had come to suspect him, but he couldn't prove anything. Without the evidence of the woman and the man who lay dead on the bed, it would be next to impossible to do so.

He crept softly to the door, opened it, and peered out into the corridor. The house was as still and silent as the man behind him on the bed. The inmates slept on, unconscious of the terror in their midst.

The murderer passed swiftly and noiselessly along the carpeted passage and down the stairs. A big stained-glass window in the great hall, which had been dark when he entered, was now glowing with colour, and he muttered an oath. Moonlight! The clouds had dispersed and the night was no longer dark. It meant an added risk. He would have to exercise greater caution to avoid being seen.

He made his way to the window by which he had gained admittance, and paused. Outside, everything was clear in the cold blue-white light of the moon, and he waited for the patrol to pass. It seemed a century before he heard the man's steps on the gravel path and presently saw him go by. The footsteps grew fainter, and faded away; and, swinging open the window, he climbed quickly out. His woollen-covered feet had barely touched the ground when he heard a shout, and realised with a sudden unpleasant leaping of his heart that he had been seen!

He spun round and saw a man hurrying towards him from the opposite direction to that taken by the first. The second watcher, tired of his lonely vigil, had come to have a word with his companion!

Behind the handkerchief that covered his face, the murderer's lips curled back from his teeth in a snarl of mingled rage and fear. Calling to his companion, the detective came running towards him. There was an answering shout from the other man, and, with a quick glance to left and right, the killer darted for the cover of the shrubbery. His movements were hampered by the thick woollen stockings over his shoes, and plunging into the bushes he stopped to tear them off. He heard the thudding of feet and the sound of excited voices behind him, and raced through the shrubbery, making for the wood. But the noise he was forced to make gave his pursuers the direction, although they could not see him, and he quickly realised that they were gaining on him. He redoubled his speed, crashing his way through the bushes, regardless of the branches that tore at his clothes and whipped his face. The concealing handkerchief about his nose and chin was caught on a twig and jerked away, leaving his hot, perspiring face exposed to the cold night air.

He reached the wire fence that divided the grounds from the wood beyond, and scrambled over. He was panting now, and the sweat was pouring down his glistening cheeks and stinging his eyes. He was not in the condition to keep up this mad pace. His heart was bounding in his breast, and there was a sharp, recurrent pain in his side that made him wince with every jerkily drawn breath. He had abandoned his original intention of paying a visit to the place where he had taken the woman. His one thought was to get away from the men whose footsteps pounded relentlessly behind him, drawing nearer and ever nearer . . .

He tried a zigzag course, blundering in and out among the trees in a vain attempt to shake them off, but they stuck grimly on his tail. There was an automatic in his hip pocket, and as he ran he tried desperately to pull it out. But it had caught in the lining, and although he tugged and tore at it he could not free it. This was the end of all his carefully planned schemes. He was to be taken like any little sneak-thief, and the mute evidence that lay in that darkened room in Chalebury Court would be sufficient to hang him . . .

The wood came suddenly to an end,

and he found himself in open country, faced by great stretches of plough and pasture land, bathed in the light of the moon. The sudden emergence from the shelter of the trees gave him a shock. There was no friendly cover here to mask his movements. He was as conspicuous as a ship in mid-ocean, and his pursuers were too close for him to double back into the wood. He raced on, stumbling over the frozen furrows and still frantically trying to free his pistol. It came away at last with a ripping of tearing cloth, and, thumbing back the safety-catch, he turned at bay. The two detectives were less than twenty yards behind, running doggedly.

'Keep away!' he screamed hoarsely. 'Keep away!'

But they came on, taking no notice of his warning.

From the squat blue nose of the pistol flashed a thin pencil of flame as his finger pressed on the trigger.

One of the running figures gave a cry of pain, stumbled, and fell. For a moment his companion hesitated, and then he came on.

Again the pistol cracked sharply, but the bullet went wide, and the man continued unchecked. Two more shots, and the second man gave a grunt and went sprawling on his face.

The murderer laughed exultantly and turned. There was a chance after all. If he could get to a railway station he might yet get away before the hue and cry was raised. He slipped the smoking automatic back into his pocket and began to walk towards the wood, trying to recover from his recent exertions. Whether the men he had shot were dead, or only wounded, troubled him not at all. He was only concerned with his own safety. The second still lay where he had fallen, but the first was trying to struggle to his feet, cursing loudly and rubbing his left leg where the bullet had hit him. And then his cursing suddenly stopped, and he stared in wonderment, for from the wood came the sound of someone singing:

'D'ye ken John Peel, with his coat so gay
He lived at Troutbeck once on a day,

But now he's gone, far, far away,
We shall ne'er hear his horn in the
  morning.'

At the sound of the old familiar song coming so unexpectedly from the wood, the murderer stopped dead in his tracks.

Out of the shadows into the moonlight came a great black horse, the pink coat of its rider making a splash of colour against the drab background; the white, deathly face expressionless and terrifying.

The wounded man on the ground gave a little gasp of fear and stared with wide eyes. The man who had shot him stared, too, but for a different reason. Just when he had been congratulating himself that there was a chance of escape, this unexpected danger had loomed up out of the night.

Andrew Renton broke off in the midst of his song abruptly as he took in the situation. Here was the man who had tried to harm Audrey — who would, but for her lucky escape, have killed her. A great anger surged through him. He had no idea that the men on the ground were detectives, but he could see that they had been injured, and he guessed the cause. Reining in his horse, he looked down at the man responsible.

'What's been happening here?' he asked sternly.

The other licked his dry lips, and his hand went to the pocket where he had put the pistol. 'Don't you interfere!' he snarled. 'This is no business of yours.'

'I think it's very much business of mine,' retorted Renton. 'Who are these men, and what have you done to them?'

'What I'll do to you, if you don't keep out of it!' was the reply. 'Clear off and leave me alone, or it'll be the worse for you.' His hand came out of his pocket, holding the pistol.

'Do you think I'm afraid of that?' said Renton contemptuously. 'I've faced worse things than bullets in my time — I'm facing a far worse thing now.'

'You've asked for it, and you shall have it!' snarled the murderer; but as his finger tightened on the trigger Renton flicked the bridle, the big horse started forward, and the bullet hummed harmlessly past his head.

Before the other could fire again, there was a chorus of excited shouts, and out of the wood burst a little crowd of men. The murderer caught a glimpse of the fat, lumbering figure in their midst, and with an oath turned to run.

'Stop him!' panted Mr. Budd. 'I want that feller for murder!'

It was Renton who answered the call. The big horse plunged forward and went galloping in pursuit of the fleeing man. The fugitive turned as he heard the thudding hooves behind him, and fired. The shot was a lucky one. It caught Renton full in the chest, and he was dead before his reeling body fell from the saddle. The horse, startled by the sound of the shot and the sudden loss of the controlling hand on the rein, whinnied, shied, and lashed out with his hind feet.

The steel-shod hooves caught the murderer full in the face, smashing through flesh and bone, and hurling him, a lifeless hulk, three yards away.

'It's lucky we know who he is,' said Mr. Budd grimly a little later, gazing down at the remains. 'You'd never be able to identify him from this. His face is smashed to pulp. If you didn't know, you'd never think that was the genial landlord of the Fox and Hounds, would you, now?'

34

Cadell Speaks

Busy men hurried through the silent streets of Chalebury; cars sped back and forth along the narrow lanes. There were lights in the windows of the Fox and Hounds, and in the windows of Chalebury Court and Oaklands. Lights, too, in many other houses throughout the district, where scared men and women, hastily awakened from sleep, were whisked away in charge of the stern-faced detectives who had come for them. The desk-sergeant in the tiny charge-room of the little police station worked harder than he had ever done before during all his years of duty, and over the telephone lines went urgent messages to Scotland Yard. It was a night of ceaseless activity for everybody concerned — activity that continued far into the coming day.

Mr. Budd was here, there, and everywhere, weary-eyed, breathless and perspiring; and the melancholy Leek, galvanised into action under the driving force of his superior, displayed an energy that was remarkable.

The sun was up, shining coldly over the frost-bound countryside, before the major portion of what had to be done was completed, and the superintendent took a momentary rest and refreshed himself with steaming coffee in Inspector Dadd's microscopic office.

'I think that's pretty nearly everythin',' he remarked with a prodigious yawn, glancing at the mass of scribbled notes in front of him. 'We've got the small fry, an' we've got what's left of the big fish. The rest of it's just an ordinary matter of routine.'

'What about Miss Renton?' asked the inspector.

'We'll attend to her presently,' answered Mr. Budd. 'She's all right where she is at the moment. How did she take the death of her father, Weston?'

Tommy, who had elected to break the news to her, crushed out the stub of his cigarette in the inspector's ashtray. 'Better than I expected,' he replied. 'It gave her a shock, of course, and she was naturally upset, but it didn't affect her as badly as I anticipated.'

Mr. Budd grunted. 'If she did but know it, it's a blessin' in disguise,' he said. 'It's goin' to save 'er a lot o' trouble once she gets over the first shock of her loss. I wish we could've taken that other feller alive, though,' he added sadly.

'I don't see that it matters very much,' said the reporter. 'He'd have been hanged in any case. The horse saved the executioner a job. What made him kill Chalebury?'

'To keep his mouth shut,' answered the superintendent. 'He overheard what Major Hankin was tellin' me yesterday at the inn, about Chalebury's visit, an' concluded that he was on the point o' squealin', which he undoubtedly was.'

'There's quite a lot I don't understand,' said Tommy curiously. 'This man Ketler was responsible for the flood of forgeries, wasn't he?'

'He was,' replied Mr. Budd, nodding gravely. 'We found the plant in the cellars of the inn — an electric press, stacks o' paper, plates, everythin'. We also found how he managed to get out without my men seein' him. He'd made a passage from one cellar to a dried-up well in a corner o' the field at the back of the pub. He could come and go whenever he liked, an' no one the wiser. I expect he originally used it for 'is Stockin'-foot impersonation.'

'What was the idea of that? If he was turning out these forged notes wholesale, and getting a huge profit out of them, what did he want to go in for burglary for?'

'That's somethin' I'll probably be able to tell you later,' said Mr. Budd. 'At the moment, I don't know.'

'And how did Chalebury come into it?' went on Tommy. 'He was in the note racket, I suppose?'

'He most certainly was. Maybe we'll all know a lot more after I've seen this feller Cadell.'

'Yes — what's his part in all this?'

For answer, the big man rose wearily to his feet. 'I'm goin' along now to ask him,' he said. 'You can come too, if you like.'

They found the novelist finishing his breakfast.

'I hear there have been stirring doings in Chalebury during the night,' he said when they were seated in the pleasant dining-room. 'Battle, murder, and sudden death!'

'That's a pretty good description,' said Mr. Budd, nodding.

'What's the reason for this visit?' Cadell asked abruptly.

'I want some information,' answered Mr. Budd. 'I want a story from you that begins several years ago, an' ends with your visit to your wife last night.'

Cadell helped himself to a cigarette, lit it, and eyed him steadily through the smoke. 'So you know about that?' he said after a pause. 'Hm, well, before I say anything, suppose you tell me exactly what happened last night.'

Rather to Tommy's surprise, Mr. Budd complied.

'So Ketler was responsible for all this trouble, eh?' remarked Cadell when the detective finished. 'That surprises me. I'd no idea. What are you going to do about my wife?'

'I'm not goin' to do anythin' until I've

heard your story an' hers,' replied Mr. Budd. 'She engraved those plates — '

'You've no proof of that!'

'No, I've no proof. But I'm sure, all the same.'

'Your conviction isn't evidence,' said Cadell. He threw his cigarette into the fire. 'I'll tell you what you want to know,' he went on quickly.

He took out another cigarette, twisting it about in his fingers without lighting it. 'I had a pretty hard time during my early life,' he began abruptly, 'but I'm not going into details, because it has very little concern with this business. I drifted about, doing all sorts of odd jobs, and making a success of none of them. It's immaterial how I came to meet Charles Ingram; the only thing that matters is that I did meet him. I was very hard up at the time — practically starving — and he got me a job. It wasn't a very good job, but it kept me in food and clothes and supplied me with a roof over my head. I was naturally grateful to him. Beyond the fact that he lived in a big house and seemed to be fairly well off, I knew nothing about him at all. I had no idea that he was a crook until some time after. I'll come to that later.

'I continued with my job, spending two or three evenings a week at Ingram's house. I met his daughter, Faith, and fell in love with her almost at first sight; but marriage was out of the question on the money I was earning, and I kept my feelings to myself. Then a relation whom I'd never seen — a distant cousin — died, and I found that I'd come into nearly five thousand pounds. It was a fortune — or it seemed so in those days. To cut a long story short, I proposed to Faith and married her.

'We spent a gloriously happy six months together — and then the bubble burst. I'd run out of money, and the banks were shut. Faith suggested that her father would cash a cheque — he always kept a large sum of ready money in the house. I went round — we only lived a few doors away — and Ingram gave me ten five-pound notes for my cheque. You know what happened. There was a flood of forgeries at the time, and I was arrested trying to change one of the notes. It was slush, and so were the rest of the notes found on me. I couldn't account for them without incriminating Faith's father, so I kept silent. I got eighteen months.

'When I'd served my sentence I tried to find my wife, but she'd disappeared, and so had Ingram. I discovered after a number of inquiries that he was dead, and that Faith had gone abroad with a man called Frank Norrington. It was only then that I learned that Ingram had been a crook, and had served several sentences for forgery. I found that the remains of my money had gone, too, and I naturally concluded that the whole thing had been a put-up job to get me out of the way, and that my wife had been a party to it. It was only last night that I discovered she'd been told I was dead, and that forged documents had been shown her to prove it.

'I was penniless and embittered. I'd lost everything, and I was filled with a cold rage against the people who'd been responsible. Ingram was dead and beyond my reach, but I swore that one day I'd get even with Faith and the man she'd fled with. I changed my name to Cadell, and started to rebuild my shattered life. I began to write, achieved almost immediate success, and found myself richer than I'd ever been before.

'I set inquiry agents to work to trace Norrington, and discovered that his real name was Sir Eustace Chalebury. He was married, with a grown-up son, and at first I thought my agents had made a mistake. But they produced proof that he and the man who had passed as Frank Norrington were the same. I could find no trace of Faith. She'd been living as Mrs. Norrington in Paris, but she'd left suddenly and completely disappeared. However, I knew where to find Norrington, and that was something. I bought this house and came to live in Chalebury with one idea — to have my revenge on 'Norrington'.

'On the night I arrived, Hickling was killed; the whole village was in a panic over the Huntsman, and since I had made no plans as to what I should do with Chalebury, I decided to lie low and watch events for a bit. It soon became evident that something very queer was going on, and I wondered if Chalebury was mixed up in it. I began to keep a watch on him, and I discovered that on certain nights various different people went up to Chalebury Court after everybody was in bed and whistled the opening bars of 'John Peel' under a certain window. They'd be rewarded for this strange serenade with a packet thrown out to them, and then hurry away.

'One night the packet broke open, and several sheets of paper fluttered out. One of these lodged in a bush and was overlooked by the recipient; and when he'd hastily collected the others and gone, I secured it. It was a five-pound note!

'I wondered for what service Chalebury was paying all these people so lavishly, and the real explanation never occurred to me until the night I recognised Faith when she came to the Fox and Hounds. It gave me a tremendous shock to see her, and I was afraid that she might recognise me. I instantly connected her presence in Chalebury with the five-pound note. The money that I had seen distributed was slush.

'That night, if you remember, Stocking-foot paid me a visit. He came to retrieve that five-pound note, which I had locked in my desk; and knowing what I did, when I heard that Chalebury was supposed to have shot himself in the leg, I was pretty sure he was the burglar.'

'You were wrong,' murmured Mr. Budd, opening his eyes for a second.

'Well, that's what I thought,' continued Cadell, 'and you can't wonder. I knew nothing of Ketler. I thought Chalebury was the prime figure in the business.'

'He was the cat's-paw,' said Mr. Budd. 'Nobody knew Ketler. We've got all the people who were agents for the distribution of this slush, an' none of 'em knew Ketler. The only people who knew him were Chalebury an' your wife.'

'And you can't prove that she knew him!' snapped the novelist.

'No; but I'm hopin' that she'll tell us. You went up to the court one night an' tried a whistlin' act on your own, didn't you?'

'How do you know that?' asked Cadell in surprise.

'*He* saw you,' replied Mr. Budd, jerking his head towards Tommy Weston. 'I s'pose you got a packet of these slush notes for your trouble?'

Cadell nodded.

'Well,' went on the stout superintendent thoughtfully, 'it's easy to guess why you got that crack on the head the other night. Ketler thought you was a detective. It 'ud be the natural thing he would think. He knew nothin' of what'd really brought you here.'

He hoisted himself ponderously to his feet. 'Let's go an' see Mrs. Langden,' he said. 'I think maybe she'll be able to tell us all we want to know.'

35

Sum Total

Faith Langden came slowly down the stairs, gave Mr. Budd and Tommy Weston a brief nod, and greeted Cadell with a smile. She was quite cool and collected, though her face was pale. 'I've been expecting you,' she said simply.

'Is there anywhere where we can talk in private?' asked Mr. Budd. 'There's one or two things I want to ask you, an' this seems a bit public.' He glanced round the spacious vestibule.

'Come into the writing-room,' she said. 'I don't suppose there'll be anyone there.'

She led the way up to the second floor and into a small room, furnished rather ornately with brocade-covered gilt chairs and spindle-legged tables. There was a desk in the window, which gave an excuse for the name of 'writing-room'.

'Sit down, won't you?' she said. Tommy

and Cadell did so, but Mr. Budd eyed the flimsy chairs dubiously.

'I really think it would be better if I didn't, ma'am,' he murmured, and she laughed. 'I've just bin havin' a talk with your husband,' continued the big man, 'an' he's told me quite a lot I didn't know before. I'm hopin' that you'll be able to do the same.'

'You needn't say anything unless you like, Faith,' put in Cadell quickly.

'But I think you'd be wiser if you did,' finished Mr. Budd. 'Ketler's dead, an' the Fox an' Hounds is in the hands of the police. We've found the printin'-press an' the paper, an' the plates. Those plates were engraved by you; but I'm not takin' any action until I've heard what you've got to say. If you're wise, Mrs. Langden, you'll be quite frank about the whole thin'.'

She looked at the troubled face of Cadell, and from it to the expressionless face of the detective. 'What do you want to know?' she asked.

'First, who was Ketler?' replied Mr. Budd. 'Second, anythin' you can tell me.'

'I'll tell you everything,' she said simply.

Mr. Budd nodded ponderously. 'That's very sensible. I don't want to make any trouble if it can be avoided, but naturally I've got me duty to do. If you're not very deeply involved in this business — well, it might be possible to keep you out of it altogether.'

'What I had to do with it was done under compulsion,' she answered.

'I was thinkin' somethin' of the sort,' said Mr. Budd. 'An' that makes a deal o' difference. Now, who was this feller Ketler?'

'He was my uncle,' she answered in a low voice. 'His real name was Douglas Ingram.'

'Your father's brother?' asked Mr. Budd, and she nodded. 'I see,' said the big man. 'An' he made you engrave the plates for these slush notes, eh?'

'I didn't want to, but he threatened to — to disclose something he knew . . . ' She reddened slowly and stopped.

Mr. Budd looked at her with a puzzled frown, and then his face cleared. 'I know what he threatened you with,' he said, and there was a trace of humour in his voice. 'He knew about your goin' through a form of marriage with this man Norrington while your husband was alive. That's it, isn't it?'

She was scarlet. 'I thought my — my husband was dead. I didn't know . . .' She stammered in her embarrassment.

'Bigamy's scarcely a crime,' said Mr. Budd. 'An' he held this over you to make you do what he wanted?'

'Yes; and then when I'd done the first plate, he said that now I was as much involved as he was, and he made me go on doing more when they wore out.' She was recovering her calmness. 'That was how he worked — by blackmail. He had a hold over all the people who worked for him, although they didn't even know him. He got Chalebury in his clutches that way. He'd got himself out of a hole by forging a transfer of shares belonging to a man who died. My uncle knew about it and forced him to act as a figurehead in the forgery organisation. He got a share of the profits, too.'

'Did you know that Chalebury was

Norrington?' asked Mr. Budd.

'Not until the night I came to bring some fresh plates for my uncle,' she answered. 'He asked me to take a message up to Chalebury Court. Sir Eustace would be waiting for it, he said. It was some instruction concerning a distribution on a big scale. Chalebury was waiting in the drawing-room and let me in when I tapped on the window. We both got a shock when we recognised each other.'

'How did he get shot in the leg?' asked Mr. Budd suddenly. 'That was the night, wasn't it?'

'Yes, I — I shot him!' Again the colour welled up into her cheeks. 'He — he tried to — to become friendly!'

'The swine!' broke in Cadell angrily. 'I — '

'He's dead,' interrupted Mr. Budd, 'an' he didn't die very pleasantly, so he got his deserts. What made Ingram rob all these places an' adopt the methods of Stockin'-foot?'

'The robberies were a blind,' she answered. 'He was searching for an incriminating piece of evidence. He supplied a lot of the

354

big houses in this district with beer and wine and spirits. In one consignment — he couldn't remember which — he'd included a bill written on a piece of banknote paper. It would've ruined him if it had been found. He adopted the methods of Stocking-foot to make it look like a real burglar was at work.'

'Did he find it?' asked the superintendent.

She shook her head. 'No,' she answered, and gave a little shiver. 'It went to Inspector Gowper. He didn't realise its significance, but he mentioned the peculiar paper to Uncle, and — and — '

'And he was killed,' said Mr. Budd gently. 'Ingram was pretty thorough in his methods. Hickling found out about the people goin' up at night to Chalebury Court, an' what they went for, an' he was killed, too.' He pursed his lips and rasped a finger round his unshaven chin. 'Your uncle must have talked to you a lot, Mrs. Langden,' he said.

'He was a very vain man,' she answered. 'He liked to boast of his cleverness. And I was the only safe person he could talk to.'

'Well, I think that's all,' said the detective, and gave a mighty yawn. 'Excuse me, but I'm feelin' a bit tired. There doesn't seem any reason why you should be dragged into this, ma'am. The real feller responsible's dead, so he can't bring you into it, an' he may as well bear the full brunt of it.'

'Then you mean I — I'm — I needn't stop here any longer?' said Faith eagerly.

'I mean you can do exactly as you please,' replied Mr. Budd. 'I may need you as a witness, but that's all.'

She looked at him with shining eyes, and then turned to Cadell. 'Do you remember what you asked me to promise you last night?' she said softly. 'I don't want to leave here alone.'

'This,' muttered Mr. Budd hastily, 'is where we make ourselves scarce, Weston!'

★   ★   ★

On the way back to Chalebury, Tommy put a question that had been worrying him for a long time. 'What first made you suspect Ketler?' he asked.

'Beer!' replied Mr. Budd promptly. 'You remember that scrap o' paper in the torch at Cadell's? That was the vital clue when you read it prop'ly. It was part of a bill from Bolsoms Breweries, Ltd. One of the items mentioned was 'I Firkin', which is a small barrel o' beer. It suggested a pub immediately. It was a wholesale bill, not a retail one, an' I found several similar bills at the Fox an' Hounds. I suppose you'll be rushin' along to see that woman?'

'I may drop in later,' said Tommy, reddening, and he hastily changed the subject. 'What did you want to take all those photographs for?'

'I wanted a picture of Ketler to send to the Yard for possible identification,' answered Mr. Budd. 'I should've thought a kid of six could've seen through that!'

Tommy Weston maintained a dignified silence.

★ ★ ★

The new landlord of the Fox and Hounds held the glass he had been polishing up to the light and examined it critically.

'You're not trying to make me believe that the Huntsman was a ghost after all, surely, Mr. Bragg?' he said. 'Why, I've 'eard the story too often to swoller that. Everybody knows that he was the father of that nice woman, Miss Renton what was married yesterday in Lunnon to that newspaper chap — '

'You can believe what you like, Mr. Winter,' interrupted Mr. Bragg with dignity. 'There ain't no monop'ly on what a man believes. I say there is somethin' about what 'appened in these parts last year that can't be explained by nateral means.'

'You always was a one for the spooks, Mr. Bragg!' said Scowby. 'I never met such a feller!'

'There ain't nuthin' that ain't been explained,' declared Perkins. 'Didn't you read all about it in the papers at the time?'

'You can't believe what they says in them things,' said Mr. Bragg disgustedly. 'The 'Untsman 'as been a legend fer years an' years. You can't tell me that they explained that away!'

'I ain't goin' ter try an' explain nuthin'

ter you, Bragg,' said Scowby. 'You're as obstinate as — '

'Listen!' said Mr. Bragg, holding up his hand suddenly, his face strained and white.

They all heard it, and there was a dead silence.

'D'ye ken John Peel with his coat so gay,
He lived at Troutbeck once on a day,
But now he's gone, far, far away,
We shall ne'er hear his horn in the morning.'

The familiar song, faint at first, grew gradually nearer.

'The 'Untsman!' breathed Mr. Bragg hoarsely. 'Now what d'yer say — '

'I'll have a pint o' mild an' bitter!' cried Yates from the doorway. 'Cheer up! What, did yer think I was — a ghost?'

THE FACELESS ONES
GRIM DEATH
MURDER IN MANUSCRIPT
THE GLASS ARROW
THE THIRD KEY
THE ROYAL FLUSH MURDERS
THE SQUEALER
MR. WHIPPLE EXPLAINS
THE SEVEN CLUES
THE CHAINED MAN
THE HOUSE OF THE GOAT
THE FOOTBALL POOL MURDERS
THE HAND OF FEAR
THE SORCERER'S HOUSE
THE HANGMAN
THE CON MAN
MISTER BIG
THE JOCKEY
THE SILVER HORSESHOE
THE TUDOR GARDEN MYSTERY
THE SHOW MUST GO ON
SINISTER HOUSE & OTHER STORIES
THE WITCHES' MOON
ALIAS THE GHOST
THE LADY OF DOOM